DWELLING

The Fine Art of Living with Joe, Alcohol, Sugar and God

Jolene Jones

DIAMOND MEDIA PRESS CO.
1-304-273-6157
https://www.diamondmediapressco.com/

ISBN Paperback: 978-1-951302-59-7

TABLE OF CONTENTS

"The wound is the place where the Light enters you."-Rumi

"A thousand half-loves must be forsaken to take
one whole heart home."-Rumi

"We come to love not by finding a perfect person, but by
learning to see an imperfect person perfectly"-Sam Keen

"Let yourself be drawn by the strange of what you
love-it will not lead you astray."-Rumi

"If you are irritated by every rub,
how will your mirror be polished?"-Rumi

"And still after all this time , the Sun has never said to the Earth,
'You owe me.' Look what happens with love like
that. It lights up the sky."-Rumi

"Gamble everything for love, if you are a true human being. If not, leave
this gathering. Half-heartedness doesn't reach majesty."-Rumi

Dear wonderful, wonderful daughter of mine,

This book is dedicated to you, my one and only child. It is my hope that as you see me embrace my shortcomings as transparently as I possibly can, you will learn even more— how worthy you are to have a life filled with love and belonging, joy and creating— and may you better understand me as well.

Love,
-Mom

"I have called you to walk a special path. I will bring the fruit to you. All you will have to do is pick it up and stay on my path for you. That is what it means to abide in Me." The people of Israel conquered the Promised Land as a result of obedience, not sweat, toil, or natural talent. In our work life call, He desires to give us fruit from our calling when we fulfill the unique purpose for which God made us. You will not have to manipulate the outcome. Abide completely in His presence and purposes for your life so you can pick the fruit he desires to put in your path. His nature is exceedingly beyond what we can imagine."

-OS Hillman (Twitter 11-10-2013)

INTRODUCTION

Dwelling is a memoir that paints relationships and addictions close-up. Using a deft artistic eye to interpret the life of the mind, this work willingly articulates how difficult it is to change damaging attitudes. It is an in- depth exploration of themes such as the roles ignorance and resentment play in preventing help-ful new addiction recovery methods. It is also a message of spiritual growth, hope, and inspiration.

CHAPTER ONE

"The wound is the place where the Light enters you."—*Rumi*

"Our relationship is not something I'm willing to throw away for any other project," Joe said to me over the phone. I love that he talks like that, and I tell him so. I thank him. He appreciates a point or two of mine as well.

I was already at a clinic by 9 am after that big fight, trying to get myself some anti-anxiety medication. I was bawling to the nurse when he called.

"Come on," he said, "it's the *me* that makes the *us*." I went ahead and listened to a whole lot more.

It took most of that evening to work through the sludge of the fight. There were only about two tokes left in that bag of weed when I mention to him, "I've been sucking on this one hitter so hard that I've swollen a ridge around the inside of my lips. I look like Angelina Jolie for Chris-sake!" That fit of laughter went pretty well.

"Do you ever think you missed your calling?"

This is why I love him. I appreciate that he notices my gifts. I've heard it said if they don't get your sense of humor, you'll always be looking for the one that does. Still…I am careful. When I saw that my leather watch band coordinated really well with my skin, I saw no sense in pointing *that* out.

Anyway… about *this* fight He'd been sitting in a bar for a good part of the day. When I arrived, he introduced me as his *roommate*.

Why the fuck am I sitting here, I think as I grab my purse and bolt. He ran after me; *I love him for that*.

"What's wrong?" he calls to me.

I keep going. I get in my car and start driving. My phone rings.

"What are ya doin'?"

"I'm mad, and I don't *know* what I'm doing," I say.

"Mad about what?"

I am stoned enough to answer truthfully. I tell him, "I felt so disrespected with the *roommate* thing—"

He cuts me off, "I'm not going to listen to that *shee-it.*"

I slap my phone shut. I already know this isn't gonna go anywhere good. I drive over to the house we're working on .... maybe to mow the lawn.... or maybe half of the lawn… as I obsess.

When I come back to the apartment, he is grinding his one hitter into its container with such a vengeance a vortex surely forms. We snark at each other.

He has some guy from the bar there now too. "I need you to help me move out of here this Saturday," he says to him more than once, making damn sure I heard it. Oh … and something about how whiny I am. *He's moving to his house … he can do what he wants, blah, blah, blah.*

I tell him to save his speeches for someone who cares.

The door *shuts loud* when he leaves. I go crash.

A week later, the positive momentum's going pretty well again. Our Sunday make-up sex was A+. Monday morning, he hugged and kissed me so nice as he left for work. I felt compelled to call out down the stairwell after him, "Jeez, you smell great, and you look good too."

"That's what I have to do to make a living…" but I could tell by his swagger that plans were in order for the bar again today sometime.

*****

Early in this relationship, I understood that he was a hard-core alcoholic/ addict…*but in recovery.* Strange as this may seem, that is on top of my *looking for* list. I am in recovery myself.

We speak the same language. Anyway, you know the story. For whatever reason, he took a drink, and here we are.

A couple different *possibly* stable guys took me out several times and dug me deeply… right off the bat when I moved here to the big city. I had every intention of being selective. But after Joe caught my interest, I just couldn't see anyone else. I still don't know if I could go for a less charismatic, though maybe more dependable guy. Joe laughs so pure and fine and free.

He made the store he managed so much fun to stop in. I found myself doing just that… more and more. I had a feeling he knew all about the world of addiction and recovery. He joked about *my* addictive personality. But so what? People *do* get addicted to my personality.

The *catch-a-movie* point came easy for us. Right there in the side isle, we laughingly struggled to figure out how to put each other's numbers into our cell-phones. And I *did* remember to ask, "Wait… do you drink?"

He hesitated for just a second, but then he said, "No."

"Wow great!"

He parked pretty far away on the first date night…thanks to my direction giving abilities…trying to find my place. He said I may as well drive to the theatre, if I didn't mind. I was pretty embarrassed about going right through a stop sign. I never even actually noticed until he nicely pointed it out after the fact. Yep! He was exposed to my lack of driving skills from the very start. I'm sure I got lost that night too.

Part of me did want to absorb Francis Mc Dormand in *Burn after Reading,* but I could tell he was focused more on processing my rigid food plan issues. Dear readers, you may as well know that of all the addictions I possess, some of which I *have* overcome, sugar haunts the strongest and the deepest in my being.

After the movie, I would have respected that he had to get up early for work the next day. I did a polite and sincere *had a great time.* Joe started to leave… but he turned around and came back. He wanted to talk more, and it is indeed a sad, sad story.

Joe's dad left when he was about two. Then came a step family scene with lots of siblings and heart-wrenching poverty. He doesn't remember his Mom telling him she loved him even once. By the time he was eleven, she arranged to send him off to work on some farm all summer.

The pain of embarrassment… for never even having the money for gym clothes and the little things at school…

seemed as fresh in his mind as if it had just happened yesterday.

Yet… he went out of his way as a child to learn about Jesus all by himself. Wow! He became an entrepreneur early on. I couldn't even keep track of all of the businesses he managed across the country. His energy is so apparent, and his big ideas are contagious. Some of them are brilliant.

On the first long *getting-to-know-you* call, he told me he was looking for a wholesome girl to go bicycling with. And… he wanted to find a good church. When I got off the call, I got down on my knees with… *"Thank you, Jesus… my heart be still."*

We saw each other daily. I got to know his dad and some siblings. Joe immediately became endeared to the developmentally disabled clients I worked with. I brought them into his store. He'd buy them all a pop or whatever. He loves giving. He took time to visit every time I came in. "Can't you see I'm talking to a pretty girl," he quipped to a friendly customer, as he'd wink to me.

We biked, paddled boated, and went to movies. By the time we got to the *windshield wiper* movie, we were comfortable enough to argue over viewpoints. Though I remember he did sigh out a "hey, let's not do this." We hit the record shop looking for a Bob Dylan favorite, grocery shopped, grilled, and all in all… life was good. His grilling skills are superb, by the way. Plus, he sings out loud… off key and often. I love it.

I think I'm falling in love.… with the ambiance of the apartment he'd kind of add on the side. He asked about the finish effect on my coffee table.

"It had a lot of chips in it so I hammered it into a kind of a soft flow and edged it."

"Wow, it turned out really nice," I replied and then chuckled, adding, "Sounds like something I'd do."

…there are wonders to be had in this relationship.

He started to kid that he should just stay on my couch each night. His naps there were getting longer and longer. Really, I found myself calmed by the peace of it all.

We discovered a great Friday night church service that absolutely rocks.

The leather jacket wearing minister just nails it every time… with top of the line comic timing to boot, and the music's almost an out-of-body experience. Our first night there, he reached over and tucked the tag of my shirt in, stepped back, and smiled. I can still feel that touch.

The essence of Art is the encounter of the artist with their world. Studies have revealed that people are able to observe more accurately when they are emotionally involved.

*****

Joe had, as he had told me, *a shoebox full of phone numbers that women had given him at his store.* Then he had added, but I was not like them. He had assessed my personal merit by putting the bits and pieces that I'd shared about myself… together. Not that we don't all do that, it's just so nice that he goes out of his way to explain his thought processes. He is analytical.

Coincidentally, we'd both read the same book, *"People of the Lie."* It's very, very deep. M Scott Peck does not apologize for being a Christian psychiatrist, but he does apologize for the many misconceptions surrounding Christianity as a whole.

It is the darkest book this author ever wrote, but he felt that he had to in order to "lead us to dissatisfaction with our current state of ignorance about the subject of evil." Funny how I have pretty much the same feeling about my rendering here on the subject of addiction.

Joe and I have similar histories: fourteen-year marriages, and we both have been divorced at least that long too. He'd only moved here about six months before I did. So… besides learning to navigate the city… we both were in the mode to start new lives. "You picked me," he said to me out of the blue one day.

"I know it," came out of me so automatically… it may be true.

"I can't believe you're single," he said early on. That got me. Later, when I noticed a vintage hard cover book called "You Can't Hurry Love" on his book-shelf, I felt my heart grab deeper. I could go on. I will. He actually talks to me.

He actually listens to me. He told me about some woman who had thrown herself at him recently in such a way that he saw it as crass. He is really *decent.*

Joe told me he would not be sexually *overt* and that women had been hurt by it, but he never gave me a convincing reason why he behaved in such a way. I wanted this to be an honest thing myself, so I let him know the issues I'd worked through. For the first time *ever*, I felt comfortable enough to tell a guy that *incest was my big one.*

He told me he'd run quite a gamut with addictions, including sex. Even though he didn't delve into details, I gave him an enormous amount of credit here for that. I realized that this admission can only mean that he did want a *real foundation.* I'd spent time being very promiscuous myself, so I thought *"oh, well."*

Strangely though…for years I'd honed a comic line in my head about how *I was looking for a sex addict that had reformed only to the point of monogamy.* Yet, for whatever reason, I chose not to share that here.

We hugged at every parting, but we didn't even kiss for a long time… sex either. Then, when it did *come up* (no pun intended), he insisted we sit down and *seriously talk through it first.* He was so gracious about it… the experience exemplifies to me the depth of his being. Joe said his big fear was *that if it didn't work out, our friendship would be gone then too.*

I tried to make some point about the difference between sex and making love. I had a feeling that did not necessarily hit home, but I get horny too.

In the exchange, before we did finally consummate, I muttered something about my body image insecurities, and he echoed insecurities of his own. But… it was wonderful. He wanted to do it under the covers. Fine with me… I am past my prime. The next day, he said he was thinking how good it felt all day; I was struck by what a gentleman he is. He let me know that I was special; though, in the most considerate of ways, Joe told me that he needed the freedom to *fun* with the girls at work, etc. I said something *like permission granted* here, I'm sure. Generous and very well-mannered describes him. Plus, he's not one to pass gas and belch around others, and wow… that is so nice. He goes outside to smoke and even tried to quit a couple different times.

Joe was excited to get a real Christmas tree. We did it up beautifully, with all the trimmings. He puts the tinsel on perfectly, one by one…this is a skill I admire but have yet to attain. It was exactly what I'd been craving all around. He went up north to meet my family too.

When my daughter had car troubles, it was like 50 below zero in that winter of 2008. To change this battery so deeply buried inside the car's inner compartment, Joe had to go bare handed to finally get at it…utterly and unbelievably freezing out. He did what had to be done. He does this kind of thing for perfect strangers, too, by the way.

Then Joe developed his own vehicle problems. I asked him if he wanted to move in with me. My apartment was much closer to his work. Plus, I didn't want to do that $1000 a month rent by myself either.

He said "*yes*" right away. For a qualifier, he added, "*as long as I never threw him out.*" Then something like *his experience with women had taught him that, sooner or later, they all will want to be done with him.*

I promised that I never would. I laid out a quick inspection of the self-fulfilling prophecy concept here only to end up just repeating— with absoluteness in my tone— that I would never throw him out.

*****

"I want to see you, know your voice.
Recognize you when you first come 'round the corner.
Sense your scent when I come into a room you've just left.
Know the lift of your heel, the glide of your foot.
Become familiar with the way you purse your lips
then let them part, just the slightest bit,
when I lean in to your space and kiss you.
I want to know the joy of how you whisper 'more."

-Rumi

*****

The two bedrooms suited us well. I am a horrible sleeper, and he snores.

But, happy day… he wakes up *whistling*. Both of us have quality taste in décor. We combine it better than most too. The work day routine settled in. Sunday mornings, we'd catch the painter show on early. Curled up lying next to him on the couch was the best.

Our spacious apartment was above a hippie/new-age bookstore. My method of carrying up groceries consisted of dividing it all up into plastic bags at the store. Then, as I took it out of my car, I'd line my arms with the handles of all those bags and trudge it up in one big load. Witnessing this, he recognized it as a maneuver honed from never really having had much help. He stepped right in to carry whatever, whenever he could.

*****

The *first* big fight we had, Joe came home in a crabby mood. He went off on me about the kitty litter smell in the apartment. I couldn't believe it. First of all, I knew it wasn't *that* bad, and secondly, he was a little short on his percent of actually doing household chores. So…I told him to *leave* . . . because I could. It was leased in my name. And because, of course, the one thing he'd asked I never do was *that*. Plus, I am only a partially recovered psycho myself. This is default behavior for me.

I remember feeling scared that he might really go, and I could not stand the thought of it. I'd lived by myself for years, so why? Clearly, I could see he was crazy, but what I had come to understand was that he was not *completely* crazy. And people, there is a difference. We patched it up.

He loves God with all his heart… I know without question. He happens to have a particular disease, and so do I. Big deal. Now it's a matter of navigating it. At this point, I do know better than to marry him. The financial burden that I suspect is involved with him precludes all that for now. I just want to love him. My credit's no good either, by the way, but I haven't completely ruled out rebuilding it.

We don't love qualities; we love persons, sometimes by reason of their defects as well as their qualities. -Jacques Maritain

*****

That first night going to the movies, I asked *if he had kids.* "Yep," he said proudly, "two boys working up in Alaska now, and my daughter will graduate from high school this spring. Their coming home for Christmas, and I can't wait." Well, they've come several times now and don't even call him. I hate that he has to endure such pain.

Then again, my own daughter can really put me through hoops too. At times, she likes to project that *I* am a real tyrant. Admittedly, I did succumb to mammoth pressures and raged uncontrollably in her very formative years. I am sad about that damage. I was in a much sicker place for that era, and she has pretty much now fled from my overloading her with too much of my raw and rash unburdening, I guess. And I hated *my* Dad for years, so part of me believes it's the generational curse of maladaptive upbringings.

The pain and estrangement that came with Joe's divorce were still very obvious. I felt the anxiety *myself* when he wasn't invited to his daughter's graduation or his son's wedding. We did crash those occasions with happy outcomes. That wedding reception night was our best night ever, I think. We danced all night. I felt so deeply loved and appreciated by him. He sang along with the radio the whole six-hour drive home… to keep me awake driving too.

Joe told me he justified picking up alcohol again *by believing it does NOT have to be total abstinence.* I wanted to believe he was right. But then, the occasional drinking turned daily.

"What the hell… let's get some pot," I said one night as we were driving down the street. We picked a guy up on the corner in front of a bar and bought some just like that. So…after ten years of abstinence from this, my drug of choice (I'd once spent 10 years stoned on), *I'm off and running on a close to a 5 month buzz.* And even more shameful to me, an almost 50 pound weight gain came with it.

*****

One night he asked me to bring the pot down to the alley behind his store. It was fun. When he had to get back inside, I whined about getting a kiss. He said, "Oh Geez, you get yours tonight." I squealed with disdain so sincerely that even I fell for it. I can play coy! He looked at me in total admiration for how well I just rolled that out…yet it *didn't work.*

I do wonder about the kissing thing with him. My best guess is that he's a *mouth breather.* Maybe he really can't breathe very well when he's kissing? Or maybe it's a long ago habit he formed to prevent close-up breath checks. As I piece together the evidence he's laid before me, it seems like it's been a lifelong ordeal with intimacy issues in general. I have a feeling women have really tried to love him.

I asked what he thought about my newly rekindled pot smoking. I see his neck muscles fill out nicely. I see his whole body rise up to answer simply, "Just control it."

I replied with a meek version of "I don't know if I can." But I noticed then why his speaking voice is so top-of- the- line. It's whole body thing for him. He is really real, at least part of the time. I've been around guys that try very hard not to reveal their true inner nature. This is not him. What he thinks… shows on him. I love that about him…*sometimes.*

And by the way, it has been said that addicts are the only real honest ones, even though we are also big liars.

*****

He's at the bar again tonight. I could go down there. I could call him. I could just go to bed. I could figure out concise wording and deliver a speech… maybe even an ultimatum. I can hardly concentrate on anything. I am contin- uously looking out the window for him to come home.

So, I think, *he's at the bar again.* It's pretty stupid of me to even be upset about it. He has an addiction… he can't *not* do this. So why do I put up with this? I know what co-dependency looks like. I am a Behavior Analyst. I saw red flags early on, and they hit me as equally as his positives did.

I got all snuggled into bed like I'm really going to be able to ignore where he might be at this hour. My body is happy to be at rest. But my mind wanted to punch his phone number in and curse out a what the fuck!

Then… he came home. He came in and told me how much he loves me and why. I am *beautiful*. There is *nothing about me that he would change.* When I get mad at him, he loves me even more… that I am *smart*…that I am *the funniest person he's ever known.* He loves me for *my longevity and endurance… my level of tolerance.*

*****

CHAPTER TWO

"The wound is the place where the Light enters you."—Rumi

I tried to open the door to his bedroom one evening and felt resistance . . . resistance like the type where a knife could be wedged into the door jam to block it from opening.

"Hey, are you blocking the door?" I inquire as nonchalantly as possible.

"No-oh-oh..." The last "*oh*" ended on an upward lilt to cover the whole range of emotion he just went through, trying not to show hurt or defense.

This *tuned-into-tone* thing is my main diagnostic tool for truth telling issues, *which is a must when dealing with addicts.* We lie to ourselves the most, incidentally, so it can really come off quite convincing.

He came out to the living room for a while and said he didn't feel good. He came back out about an hour later and asked if I wanted to go to church that night.

"Yes, awesome. I'd love too."

"Yeah," he says, "It's time we go." We went, but it fell flat. The regular minister wasn't there. We came back home feeling lackluster.

*****

Time goes by, and then I just couldn't get myself feeling okay about going to my part-time job one day. I obsessed in my head about it for hours. Finally, on my way to work, I decided to turn off for a garage sale *instead.*

Quite a while after I should have been working, I got a call. "Are you coming in?"

"No. No, I'm not. I quit yesterday. I left a message on the machine."

"Wow, we didn't find a message."

"…so, I guess take care."

Click.

We did get a slamming workload there a few nights back. No one's fault, but I picked up enough hints to know that if it's a scapegoat they must have, I'm the most convenient. So, I guess . . . grow up. Move on. Anyway, I do still have a good full-time job. I know better than to run without my own money.

I told Joe I quit my part time job, how and a little why. Even though we weren't in an especially close mode at the time, he *wanted* to sit down with me and to talk it through. He immediately realized the *pit of the stomach unease* of this for me. He lets me know that he's done this type of thing several times himself.

*****

So… moving on to a day when Joe said he'd be home by 2:30. Now it's 6 o'clock. I've already done my required *courtesy* check-up calls. Evidently, *something* is more interesting than me. I could torture myself with visions of him being caught up with the new women he just hired. "Man, she's perky," he said yesterday. This is something that I could really work into frenzy. But my new calmer self thinks that *letting it go* will pan out much better. Maybe I shouldn't even tell him I scored some more weed.

I also decide *not* to tell him that the guy he sends me over to buy dope from has a version of this theory himself. "Wow," the guy says to me, "Joe's got it all, man. Usually, guys think they kind of have to settle, but geez, how's the guy get so lucky to get you?"

I behave myself.

Just as an interesting side note though, I remember the first time Joe took me over to this dealer's apartment. I was shocked to learn that this big black dude was also a mainstay youth worker at his church…whatever, I guess. And I remember us having conversations on God where I'd try out my wisecracks about how *using a steady diet of Christian music might off-set all the other evil addictions…kind of like me drinking diet coke with my candy bars.* Actually, that is a concept I understand on a certain level.

Finally, Joe calls. "Hey…what-da-ya-doing?"

"I'm writing the great…"

"The great American novel?" he finishes in harmony with me.

"Yeah, that."

We "hee-hee." I am so happy that he's so happy. I am easily able to fall into smooth dialoguing abilities.

"I did laundry, and then I went and got some weed. I smoked it. Then, I ate a lot. Now my tummy really hurts."

I pause to let him chuckle and remember how *he* just did that. And because I knew he would go straight there with it, it was a safe way to *pretend* that I was being above board… meaning my tummy ache was *only* from the amount I was admitting too.

You're as sick as your secrets, we say.

We both know… *that we both know*… that particular idiom. We drag it out to use when we feel like covering up something with a *partial* truth. Then we act kind of noble about it to boot… pretending to lay our cards on the table to create some sort of pseudo honesty.

I felt a case of the warm fuzzes coming on, and I go on a nice *high* emotional binge with it. I am an addict, and it's what we do. Still, to finally at least *begin* to understand what dealing with addiction is… is a breakthrough of untold merit, by the way. Addicts are very neurotic. But we do have gifts!

Example: Joe and I were out on a drive. He gets going on his discourse about my driving. This time, it went something like, "I have to say that your driving skills have gotten so much better. Really… you were so horrible. You rode right up on the ass of the car in front of you." He rolls out a few more ditties like this, completely pleased with himself for being so complimentary. "No, no… I have to say it is so much better; you were sooo bad."

I can't stand that I am actually enjoying this— *"Oh my God!* OH MY GOD! I can't take it. I can't take anymore!" I lament out my now downed window. "God, please, please take me away. Just let me go spiriting off into the sky."

"The car would just be guided along with no driver?" Joe asks with wonder.

"Geez, you can take the car. I don't care."

"Well, no, I' d let your daughter have the car."

"She wants the dresser set I painted too." I blurt out as I'm rising up from the car seat, poised to lift off through the window. "And remember, I told you one time, I really want the song *'I'll Fly Away'* at my funeral."

"Okay yeah… I remember that." I could tell that he did or now *would at least try to.* *"Course,"* he added in a tone he had honed seemingly to support side-ways checkups referencing the state of the relationship in general. I was pretty dang happy the rest of that day.

"Just for today I will try to live this day only and not tackle my whole life problem at once. Just for today I will be happy. Just for today I will adjust myself to what is, and try not to adjust everything to my own desires. I will take my luck as it comes and fit myself to it."

-Author unknown

*****

As most nights fall, I try to focus on whatever I can to *not* keep going back to look out on the empty street. Part of me *is* happy to sit and read and listen to music. I know it will be solid History Channel when he gets home until he passes out. He'll come in with some story. "A guy came in my store tonight… and *whatever, whatever."* I hear *"My* store…" the low self-esteem… the need to puff up… I just let it ride.

Even though the house we are moving to is smaller than our apartment, Joe wants me to bring *all my stuff.* He still fills my car up with gas. He continues to hand me money to go buy anything I want. He does ask to know how my days go. He has ironed shirts for me. He takes out the garbage. He has arms and legs that wrap wonderfully around me on the couch. I love to hear his voice.

Still, I have wrestled back and forth about doing this move. I cannot call the landlord here one more time and tell him I've decided to stay. We need to be out in a few weeks, *and so we will.* He is buying his Dad's house, and we have it almost gutted. It will be like camping for a while. How long that *while* is… remains to be seen. I'm on a big adventure here. I should have walked away from this long ago. Yet, I've seen him down on his knees, praying to God to help him several times.

I cannot help thinking: *"This metamorphism is several painful experiences away from being finished."*

*****

Now for this next fight. It had crossed my mind that he could get his new drinking buddy…some ex-*mortician*…to live here at the house and come up with money to cover extra costs, just as well as I can. Plus, then they could pull off an *even more exciting drinking spree* for while… so maybe it's best for me to *not* go ballistic. Anyway, right around 1 am, Joe saunters in.

"Ooooo… you're up…Oh, waiting for me." Not a question. His recognition of shit-storm potential tells me he's been around this block a time or two. Yet, he's in his *happy mood,* so he erringly starts to chat about his evening.

"Wow, they had a great band at the bar for Halloween."

Fuck it. I came unglued. If he wants to regale, then by God… we'll regale. I sometimes use dramatic outbursts to communicate those issues of such a precarious nature that seemingly no *tactful* method of delivery is possible. Big mean verbalizations ensue. But hey, it's a great time to lay out festering points of major contention, right?

I am a long-time student of the 12 steps program's way of life, and I know I am not to take another's *inventory.* However, since I have not been working a tight program for quite a while now, I have lost a great deal of my hard-won serenity. The concept of *speaking in love* is currently lost on me. I welcome the opportunity to go off on him. I can still be as self- righteous as they come.

I reel off a list of wrongs… with academy award winning *venom* precision.

This probably comes as no surprise to those of you out there with insight into addiction. We spend inordinate amounts of time in our own heads re-working every angle of defense and invent new combinations besides. Survival skills like these do need some serious redirection. One trick is to learn to metabolize the pain and use it as positive energy.

But on *this* night, I decide that it falls to me once and for all to impress upon this fully grown man that his sometimes drunkenly and sometimes sober lines he loves to soapbox about— b*eing a man of principle, codes and ethics—* CANNOT continue.

I don't remember exactly how he used the concept here, but I'd been laying in wait over it. I've smoked so much pot that it is easy for me to override any stoppers now that would take his fragile psyche into consideration. I calculate that trying later to write it off as being REALLY stoned…to possibly be the *only* way I will someday be forgiven for the message I deliver to him. *"Jesus Christ! I just want to STAB you every time I hear you even start with that bullshit.* I've heard it on every psych ward I ever worked on. What ethic is it to drive drunk?"

"Did you just threaten me? Don't you threaten *me!*"

I lash out. *"I'm going to go stay at my brother's house. I'll get my stuff on my days off."* Saying this to him almost requires more effort than I have. I am bone and soul tired. I just got unpacked from moving over here. I flounce back to lay on my bed, and I hear mocking tidbits.

"Brother! Brother! *Waa, Waa."* I find this semi-entertaining as I know he really thinks very highly of him, and it serves to illustrate his level of inebriation. I come back out to hear him say, *"You don't come get your stuff unless I'm here."*

To that, I say, *"You can have everything…"*

And sick as it is… I know this is not going to break us up and that for whatever reason, God wants me here with him.

What is the principle in play here? Maybe whoever is the nastiest is the loser regardless of the rights and wrongs. I'm aware of that— possibly even use it so that he *can* save face—but I know the real message got to him... mean, mean shit that I can be. He is a man of great principle when he's sober and tries damn hard to be when he's drinking too.

So, I guess you know how this is going to go. Three more weeks of almost round the clock drinking before he finally utters, *"If I had a gun, I'd shoot my-self."* Actually, we are both happy. The totally out-of-control came as fast as it did.

"Thank you, Jesus" is all I can utter, as he lets me get him checked into a hospital.

*****

Throughout *that* month and a half of treatment, he loved me uncondi-tionally. I knew he was filled with humility and trying his best. It was another extremely cold winter. The guys had to go outdoors to smoke. Those traces of his tears, chapped and etched into the skin below his eyes, are now forever in my memory.

He got a pass to give me a Christmas present...a dainty silver circle on a chain. *A circle's round and has no end, that's how long I want to be your friend.* He put it on me in the car in the parking lot and kissed me really, really well. And if I let myself, I can still feel *that* tender rendering in its place in my soul. "Let's get a nice professional photo done together too," he said.

I wore that necklace almost like it was a dog tag, no matter what was going on with us after that. But I also remember what it was like when I had to twist, pull, and pry to get my wedding ring off my fattened finger many, many years prior. The *real* pain was the emotional knife I felt as I hurled that at my now ex-husband. I remember it *as the finality* of a 14-year relationship.

Anyway, after Christmas there were lots of bad attitudes going around that treatment center. Poor staffing, and Joe was one of the only white men there. He was asked to leave shortly after that because of some really insignificant issue. But... he wasn't drinking. He was attending meetings, and I thoroughly enjoyed going with him. And on a side note: My dentist, who went to some of the same meetings, told me *it's pretty crazy when two addicts live together just so you know.*

After a big struggle to find employment, Joe finally caught a break doing painting and carpenter work. His dad transferred all the paperwork for the house over to him, and Joe had a house to call his own. Many times, it is the high points in life that really get addicts in trouble… *those hard to handle highs and lows.*

So, one morning shortly after that, Joe announced that he was going to a meeting that night and that *he didn't want me to come with.* He tried to suggest a guy time picture that didn't wash because he'd been doing plenty of that lately.

I was stunned… I just left for work early, without saying a word. When I got home, I showered and put on my nightgown to let him know I had *no intention* of begging to come along. We didn't speak. I went in my bedroom until I heard him leave. I came out to such a *wave of aftershave* and snapped.

I hit his number on my speed dial.

"What?" he snarled.

"I want to talk."

He launched into some bullshit about how he doesn't need this kind of drama in his life, so I hung up. A few minutes later, he called back. "Did you just hang up on me? I was talking to myself a good three minutes before I even realized you had hung up. That is so disrespectful."

"Yeah," I exploded, *"so is using so much aftershave that you smell like a* WHORE."

I slammed my phone shut. I knew I should have called a sponsor to talk me down all that day, but I didn't because I wanted to go off on him. I was hurt. This apparently is the only comfort I know.

All this *drama—* as he calls it— because he wanted to go an AA meeting without me. It was more than that I know, and he even later admitted it was to give a gal a ride. But… I made it worse. God give me direction, I pray. I got dressed and drove around, trying to calm down. I called my daughter. She would let me stay overnight if I insisted, but she really advised against opening *that door*. How did she get so smart, I wonder?

"I would give anything to have someone care about me as much as you two care about each other," she tells me. She also points out that, as my daughter, she is fully aware of my hurtful communication style... that "heads up, it doesn't work." Her recommendation was that I journal about why I love him and stay calm.

He was in his room with the lights out when I got back. I wrote a note, "I am sorry I went off on you," and taped it to the toilet lid before I went to bed. When I used the bathroom later, it was crumpled on the floor.

*****

I have the house to myself today, and it's raining. I have Jazz music on. I tried to apologize before he went to work...to no avail. Evidently, he *likes* feeling injured. I had managed to slide key points in, so all would not be lost for the mulling period. He'd been referring to us as common law lately...so I have a basis for the level of commitment he abused. But I also think he may be hurt that I do not want to marry him right now.

He is being *very* obstinate. I'm starting to think maybe I really *did* have a part to amend to. What a revelation. I was actually thinking my side was *A-okay* earlier and that I needed to make amends. *Just to do it.* Now I see that I really did hurt him. So, here I am, hopefully at a breaking point for another of my shortcomings.

All the next day sucked too. I walked around the house, finding reasons why we belonged together. He got the house from his Dad. I had brought some of my neat old family heirlooms. We both collected old blue-glass. Everything we needed fit together on a shoestring. It's as cozy as cozy gets. It is surreal that it's so right.

The *next* day, I'm up at 5:30 am, even though I have it off. Everything is still tense. I get dressed and then lay back down on my bed. I get this idea that I really could just take some food, clothes, and my laptop and go. My brother and his wife would welcome me, and it's close to my work.

21

Wow, that's a really scary thought. I *better get up right now and start journaling or something just to get my head screwed back on right.* OK… I'm up and at the keyboard getting it down… getting it out.

He gets up.

"Morning," I say like we do every day.

He says *morning* less than friendly.

I think that he's milking this for all it's worth. He settles into the recliner. I start feeling pretty brave because I did work out an approach in my head earlier. It's the method of hedging into being *kind of sorry* for what I said, but of course, then *turning it enough* to present some new food for thought to him.

I admit this here because it portrays the addict's thinking *I still suffer from.* But at this juncture, I want to believe that my formerly troublesome character defect of brooding and obsessing has now been transformed into a possibly *divine gift,* whereby I can provide and project the perfect understanding into his brain.

For example: I could say, *I'm sorry what I said hurt so much. In fact, I'm not even sure exactly what I did say.* Then, I could add in a rush and a flush, *All I know is that what you were saying didn't add up.*

Then, also because I'm an addict, I could launch into a *seemingly* unrehearsed performance where I torrent out the evidence I have stacked against him. I am thinking along these lines because I want him to know that I know he is not innocent. This is for his own good more than to *just take his inventory…* noble soul that I am.

"Can we talk?" I ask.

"About what?" he asks.

"Us…"

I hear some version again about how I am so disrespectful. I'd hung up the phone on him two nights ago. He heads into his room. I follow him.

He snarls, "You can't come in my room!"

I come unglued. "Fuck *this* shit," I say, "I'm leaving."

I surprise *myself* as these words come rolling out of my mouth. The momentum has started, and I cannot stop it. I become resolutely collected about it. All business. I grab big plastic bags and start throwing in essentials. I don't even forget to bring the bills I pay.

"I'll get my furniture later."

"Leave the keys."

"No problem."

Half way through all the trips out to the car, he quietly says, "You don't have to leave."

"I don't want to," I manage to mutter.

We are now conversing at our truest level. We are saying what we think in our hearts. There's no contrived thought to it. I am honored he said what he just did. Still, I come back with, "I can't live with someone who doesn't love me." This is choked with real. But I just keep loading up my car.

He is in an almost fetal position in the recliner. I see the pain. Yet, his story just didn't add up. He still likes his *ego* stroked by any skirt that comes along willing to do it. AA meetings are as good a place as any, so suddenly, I'm not invited to come along. I have dealt with a lot of his shit, but I just do not want to tolerate this level of disrespect.

"Sorry, it didn't work out." My parting words on the last trip out the door. I drive away. I am almost to my brother's house, 45 minutes away, before I even have the guts to call and tell them I'm coming to move in.

*****

Joe is who he is. He is who I fell in love with. There is an upside to the super sensitivity of addicts. It is a scientific fact that we have lower beta-endorphin levels, which means we are less insulated. Translated, this means we do have a different kind of awareness, compassion, and intuition. Pain is felt deeper, and so is pleasure. I started thinking about Joe pointing out how neat or interesting or cute so many things are, and how I feel far, far behind him in the *living in the moment* department. So, I called to tell him *I love him* from my brother's house.

"Whatever."

It could go either way. I think his biggest temptation is that now he has a place to call his own and wants all the avenues open to go with it. I don't think it's really about me. Whether or not he loves me, he probably needs to say that he does not… when he wants to act like a slime-ball around other women … just to get a perk. And even worse, he feels the need to act like this to impress the other guys.

This is all so adolescent, I know. Though having met later in life, if growing up ever does happen for us, *I wonder if it should be comparable to having known each other since our teenage years.*

I am not at my brother's very long before I fully realize I need my own kitchen to operate efficiently. A few days later, when Joe calls for help with a flat-tire, I come to the rescue.

While I'm at it, I *grovel* to move back in. He cries with me and agrees I can come back but *only as a roommate,* and he did also say *it needed to be that way for my own good.*

Now I've had a chance to take a step back and look hard at this situation. In all honesty, he really has presented with both sides of his personality all along. But because his charming self was so charming, I didn't really let his other self… *register.* I was determined that we had enough significant spiritual and psychological *in-tune-ments*… I guess.

And I believed that since we had both already had such hard lives, the fact that we were even willing to try to couple-up was an additional indicator of fate. But, as addicts, we do have dual personalities, thus the Jekyll and Hyde syndrome. While I continued to believe that the positives were all true, *it didn't really mean that the negative ones weren't true as well.* In our case, it has factored out to look like a Love/Hate scenario many times.

Several times now Joe told me about spending the night at some gal's place on the couch. When he never made it to the bedroom, in the morning she told him how offended she was, etc. He told me this, I think, because he is aware of some of his issues and of the pain they cause. Also… as I look at our situation, it seems like the trouble started after we instigated a sex life.

The thing is though… *it was always him trying to stay overnight on the couch that made me want to ask him to move in with me in the first place.* He is lonely, and he actually does want a relationship— *and so do I.*

Anyway, I moved back in, and I am still completely *unaware* that someone suffering from sexual anorexia/sex addiction and the continuum there-in really can *only* view successful intimacy as another window to possible betrayal. Also… a lot of sexual betrayal survivors see intimacy as having an exploitative agenda. Therefore, they put up barriers to keep their vulnerable self safe. They don't accept anything that could create the chance of being hurt again.

Of course, this anxiety-free state where they feel no hurt does not last. A core empty loneliness gives way to hopelessness. This often leads to abusing a substance or obsessing to try to block those feelings. Self-hatred torments them because they feel so flawed. In his case, it *really* comes off as a waste because he is playful *and* sensuous, all rolled up together.

So … *now what?* I am here because I choose to be, but it isn't fun for me. Yet, I feel like I am supposed to be here. On days when it seems like maybe I've sacrificed too much, I think of that lady who lived with apes for many years just to study them. Believe me, this is a study in many things. A creative life involves great attention as a way to connect and survive.

I am also aware that the process of interacting in relationships is also a mirror to our own selves. I have not yet begun to understand exactly what is allowing me to consider such a pattern of avoidance on my part. I have let my food program slide into relapse. That is about me. If I'm not in recovery, I won't be in a decent relationship with anyone, including myself.

"Your task is not to seek love, but to seek and find all the barriers within yourself that you have built against it." –Rumi

CHAPTER THREE

"We come to love not by finding a perfect person, but by learning to see an imperfect person perfectly"- Sam Keen

I spend most of my summer free time working on art projects that teach me more about serenity. I have now been introduced to recycling centers down here that supply me with free paint. I do a mural across the back yard retaining wall. While it is not quite the Mt. Rushmore *scale of grand*, it did surpass my own expectations. I learn on a deeper level that art is also about renewing and transforming the mind. As I draw closer to my creative source, I find that it is also a wonderful fount for discernment and knowing the truth.

I am an artist. And that can also mean I have a tendency to reveal underlying spiritual and psychological conditions. Plus, I am able to take something I have access to and use it in a valuable place. I am capable of at least partially transforming what could be truly depressing into something brighter. It is peaceful to start learning to trust my own inner voice.

I've read it takes a good year of sobriety for relationship to get on an even keel. Now at five months, we got to talking about show on television, and one thing lead to another, and I heard him accidentally slide in *Oh Hon, I'm sure that did hurt.* Things like that help a lot.

I haven't smoked pot now since Joe went to treatment, November of 2009, though I am still not running my food program as tight as I'd like too. I will stop right now and pray for the willingness. This is an area I can be a witness in for generations to come. *"God, grant me the power to carry out your will for me. Amen."*

It's a good thing I'm in a strong place right now. I went up north to my Mom's, and Joe called to see *what time I'd be home.* I found an empty 12 pack in the trash I figured would be there when I got back. I suspected what was happening by his raging mood swings. He has set himself up in a house painting business and is starting to make a good money again.

"Somehow I always manage to come out smelling like a rose," he says.

"Wow, maybe you are rose." I say, probably, to deaf ears.

*****

Some days it really is too much. I am sickened by website details I've found on my computer. I conveniently forget about the shit I've looked at myself, I guess. I think I never want him again. He is what he is. Dear God, forget about helping him, *help me, help me.* Please get me out of here. Wow...

I've set up the basement to function as a get-way. Here I am at three in the morning trying to get this all down. I have tomorrow off, and I need to find an Al-anon meeting for sure. I need to do an even better job of detaching emotionally... even though *I do know* the badmouthing he does *to me* and *about me* is his alcoholism. I *also* know... God puts us in places he needs us to be and that He will save me from scarring.

Months now of almost daily drinking and all the typical side effects that go with *being active* in the disease. Bullshit bar floozy slime behaviors. Throwing money around like there is no tomorrow. Bragging, grandiosity, and blaming. I pray to see him as a person first...*trying* to cope with a *disease*. I think it is a lesson. I don't know if I've reached true emotional equilibrium yet, but I *have* been able to listen to Bonnie Raitt and not feel the pain... to be specifically for me... *anymore.*

He was on a week-long drinking binge at his brothers over Thanksgiving. I worked out a painting depicting a shepherd *training a sheep to stop straying.* As the story goes, the shepherd breaks the sheep's legs and then carries it around his neck. During the time it takes to heal, the lamb becomes so used to being close to his shepherd; it never wants to stray again.

I felt like since *the good shepherd is in us, the face of this shepherd should reflect the people looking at it.* I managed to get my upper portion and Joe's lower portion... *of our faces* co-mingled together pretty well on a shepherd's body in this piece of art. Working on it carried me through all those days of him doing *God knows what.* I hung it on his bedroom door. He ragingly kicked it to the basement when he got home.

*****

I regain my equilibrium and manage to feel grateful. Living here has actually been the most secure I've felt financially *since I don't even know when.* I pay the utilities to have access to everything. I get a yard complete with flower beds *he has made for me.* There's just enough room off the alley for my motor home to even look rather park-like. I have a basement semi-art studio and my own bedroom. And it's been a long time now that I haven't needed a second job.

I have enough free time to pursue my interest. I am able to work on many creative things. Much of this is because Joe is who he is. Mine is the bigger bedroom, and bulk of the household stuff we kept is mine. He does this for me because *it is what he can do for me.* Even though he does flare to polar opposite moods, his core self is looking to make a difference where he can. Many times when we pull up to the house, we do pause to look over all the work we've done on the place and then say, "It is good."

Now the third year we're together, Joe started talking about a fabulous Christmas gift to me by suggesting diamond earring. "At least a half-carat... Sport them!"

Then... he went on to lay out his *other plans* for Christmas. It felt like toss me that bone to justify running off on a week-long drunk and leaving me to fend for myself. My response to the earrings offer was to question his *driving a vehicle...without a license...drunk.*

"Wow," he said, "Wow." He was again genuinely hurt.

I apologized, *admitting* that his offer was *the nicest present I've ever even been considered for.*

So...he gave me *nothing.* He wouldn't accept the presents I had for him either. He bought up a bunch of presents for some distant relatives and left for days on end.

I do get a lot of stuff done when he's gone, at least. I've been divorced now since 1991, so holidays being nothing special are more common than not. Plus, I have started to wonder about women, like Abigail Addams, who excelled, and I think her man was gone a lot too.

I ran across an article explaining how some guys totally get into *pumping up* how much the gal is going to love some gift, or vacation, or whatever. These things usually do not transpire. The lesson here is *that the real gift is the sheer grandiosity of their intentions.* The point was to accept that and appreciate the small things they do as the grand declarations of love *that they are.* Tell him you love him no matter what… and take the pressure off of it for him.

Food for thought here, anyway. I can see how the level of poverty in his youth could have played a role in producing this kind of almost intentional substituting, kind of like the people that get more fun out of planning a vacation than taking one.

*****

He's pretty broke now after throwing around in the bars and Christmas bullshit. No real work lined up at this point either. One Monday morning, I was getting ready to re-tile the seats on some great patio chairs I'd scored free on Craigslist.

He left the house saying, *"I'll bring home that grouting tool you wanted tonight."*

He didn't come home that night. He didn't come home one night the week before either. When I called him *that* next morning *to see if he was still alive,* he said, "Course I am." He came right home then. He even joked to me about small hole in his dress socks. As in, *oh my, what must she have thought?* I am numb with pain.

In a phone call to his niece that night, he made sure I'd hear. "Don't worry about the ugly scrum-bags I've been hanging with… I found a new lady *that reminds me of my ex*… and what a *joy* she is."

When he got off the phone, he told me in no uncertain terms not to *ever* call him again before 8 am. *"How do you think I felt* getting a call when I was *LAYING IN SOMEONE ELSE'S BED?"* he screams to me.

This time now, I did not see or hear from him again… until *four* nights later. I am in the shower getting ready to go to another Al-anon meeting when I hear him call out, "I'm home!"

"Did you bring the grouting tool?" was the best I could find to say.

"I did." He replied, sounding very proud of himself. I could smell alcohol seeping out of every pore as he crashed in the easy chair to an almost instantly thunderous snore.

Later, he tried to nudge up with me as I was doing the dishes. He must have *forgotten* his mandate that I'm not his girlfriend anymore. He even offered to bring me a glass of soda. *My* …how well-mannered he must have been with her.

I don't let my almost *suffocating pain* show here either.

I relayed *that* scene to my sponsor, and she dropped me the next day. It was too close to the excruciating scenes she deals with herself. I was so full of pain already, anything else— like suddenly having to find another sponsor too— couldn't really feel much worse.

But at least now when he tries to pursue *having girlfriends* as something that will somehow be what he needs to *feel better* and acts out almost beyond belief… *I have come to realize*… he probably isn't going to bring them here or throw me out. I have also come to believe even this particular avenue is too much for him, most of the time. He's got some knocks without my saying a word. God orchestrates it. I'm learning.

*****

I had to file bankruptcy after I moved down here, mostly because I couldn't sell the house I had up north when I got better job. Then, being the lower middle-class working fool that I am, I didn't even qualify for a Chapter 7. This means I had to do a Chapter 13 judgment, with an extra $450 payment on me for five years. It also means that it will be *years* yet before I can even qualify for loans, etc.

But I am more than surviving. By the grace of God, I am able to somehow see the challenge in whatever light there is. I have just touched the tip of the creative world here in the big city. I try to divide my time into useful and satisfying activities. I know that even if I only play a small role, I can make a difference.

Joe's addiction is a powerful picture for me… *of being trapped in pain.* Miraculously, it has turned into the main deterrent for me, and to continue to abstain at least from alcohol and drugs myself. I've studied addiction. It is real. It is not their fault. He has told me that chances are he was even born an addict. This could very well be. His family is riddled with alcoholism and addiction. It is common for addicts to have the emotional level of a teenager by the way, regardless of their IQ. Some wise minds have suggested an approach of loving them into sobriety.

*****

The winter goes by. He's been decent…*more than I would think possible* for the level of addiction he appears to be at. He came back from his rendezvous *several* degrees nicer to me. We actually watch movies together again now. I have him believing the movies are just a *random* selection from Netflix. During the illicit affair scene in one movie, he muttered, "Oh, what a mistake."

One day he finds it necessary to ask my thoughts about his behaviors.

"Okay," I say with a tone that he'd be able to read *as you did try to warn me about this tendency early on,* "I believe you do have sex addict issues along everything else."

He somberly nods to that.

I have told people for years that I have an affinity for the sick and twisted. Now when people ask what I do, and I'm in the smart-ass mood, I sometimes go ahead and tell them that *I am a Behavior Analyst.* This works out well when I sense someone is along, prodding me to define my relationship with Joe. I come back with a quick smirking, *"and he's a case."*

Shit-head that I can be.

*****

Summer rolls around again. My neighbor lady asked me *when* we were going to move the gigantic pile of dirt we left on her property last fall. She was pretty nice about it but ended with a very stern look. I told Joe about it…so we would get it moved *soon.*

The next day, he went off on her for that… and a few other neighbors for various things. Drunk, of course. Then when she apologized to me *if she'd been harsh,* it was also really about questioning why Joe had come down so hard on her. I just spoke the truth. "He suffers greatly from alcoholism, you know."

She didn't know… but then *did* seem to understand. Chances are she too has been exposed to someone such as this. Someone that can be kinder than words can ever say… then to devastate with their next mood sway.

Surprisingly though…what she took away from his barrage was *how much he cares about me.* Well, I know the ebb and flow of that. She's a single career girl and very pretty. It was interesting to me *that* was what was most interesting to her.

"Something must have happened to her… to still be single." He said.

I'm thinking chances are good she was raised with some alcoholism around her, too. But I'm not going to tell him that I clued her in *because* there is so much shame involved in it. So, maybe, a purpose of my writing this is to clue in whoever chooses to read it.

*****

I tried to like other guys here and there along the way too. But I couldn't get into it. I must love Joe, which is a good fact to know but a hard one. I have known it all along I guess… because I have stood over him wondering how to love him and *wanting* to love him better than anything he's ever known.

I've only had that one 5-month pot-smoking relapse in 12 years of recovery. This relapse proved that I cannot ever safely pick up, much as I wish I could at times. *Still,* even after I had that lesson driven home to me, I almost did it one night again. Some neighborhood guys helped put new carpet in the cab of my motor-home, and it became a sort of christening party. The pot came out, and I wanted to be in the *camaraderie.* Joe stopped me. "No," he said, "I've seen what happens to you, and you can't … so don't pick it up at all." It was not to be mean, but just knowing what would happen, as only addicts know. And then the urge just dissipated. Thank you, Jesus and Joe.

Time goes by, and I am grateful *now* that every day I can walk a little better on my newly rebuilt metal knee. I had to have one of my artificial knees re-done. Here, I am compelled to point out for you to please note that it turned out to be *my leg* that was broken…*remember my painting?*

I was able to get a nice laptop cheap and then make another little retreat in my Craigslist Motor-home find. To re-do the outside finish on that, I had to squeeze between the neighbor's garage and cramp arm paint the strokes. But thank you, God, I managed. This serves as a testament for *where there's a will, there's a way…* like when I start thinking I don't have enough space inside this little hovel of a house we live in to spread out the way I think I should to write.

*****

I have learned a lot from Al-Anon literature this last year. I need to think honestly and in depth about my attitudes and surrender to God's guidance. I finally understood that I was a drug addict many years before I understood that I was also a food addict. Now I understand being well a lot better. I will focus on doing my food right and trust that whatever changes I need to make will become clear to me over time. I am a woman doing my best… to beat my crippling addiction. I want to be an overcomer!

I am not squandering my days harboring resentments. I seek out spiritual growth. Theoretically, at least, I avoid arguments and retaliation. I do not live in fear for very long these days because I know when my thoughts are distorted by resentments or despair, I cannot make wise decision. I trust my higher power to direct me. I am trying to not be selfish or inconsiderate, and when I am, I do try to make amends as soon as possible.

*****

I am still living with Joe, who is still a practicing alcoholic… and still *not* my boyfriend… by his directive. I am *not* his type, he tells me now. This has been his stance for so long now that I can see where the sheer amount of times he has repeated this sentiment has worn a path in his brain convincing him of it. I choose to just *leap over the tiresome game* in general.

Basically, I know that if he doesn't end up working a tight recovery program, in the end, this *won't* work out, and if he does, then why even discuss what is essentially just disease fodder? But time will tell, and God is in the details.

Joe is a slender, mostly bald man, who is also captivating and good looking. He is the very nice brand of bald. He does not hide it under a hat. The crown of speckled freckles is completely endearing. His *gait* has a sway of confidence about it. His *posture* carries with determined internal command, like a plant that grows to be so splendidly graceful from some seriously un-godly terrain. In fact, he did give me a photograph of himself that is awesome. A professional photographer had come into his store and asked to do a session for free on him because *he exudes so much character.*

I'm a beautiful and shapely gal for my age, a little saggy, but believe me, I've looked worse. And upon closer inspection, you'd also see degenerative arthritis in my hands, and the beginning of a farmers stoop starting in my lower back. Here, I hold out that the masses instantly become educated about concepts held towards Joshua trees. Their almost ugly silhouette not only tells a story of survival, resilience, and beauty borne through perseverance, but if you live around them, you know you are home when you see them.

Anyway, if *I* were to have a specified body *type* I was attracted to, I supposed it would be a more substantial male.

Not that he's not well endowed, just slighter of overall build. But I am an *equal opportunity* thinker, and he had other redeeming factors that were more important. We are in our fifties, after all.

But at the moment, I'm not feeling much love. I'm sick to death of the loadie scene here. The homeless guy *that Joe did politely ask if it was alright with me to have stay here* has been staying on the floor of our dive basement all this summer. He's been working with Joe, and they hit the bars daily. Therefore, Joe also has to make sure he states regularly how single he is.

While it seems as though everything Joe has to say to me these days serves only as some sort of statement that I am nothing to him, what about the *intake* conversations at the on-set of this relationship? Specifically, the conversation where we admit to each other that we are fully aware of true context of the: *me think-eth you protest-eth too much* adage?

The house is a toxic mix of the dirty Mexican, (the guy in the basement's self-definition), cigarettes, pot, alcohol, and burnt cooking. Add to that non-stop television droning on and on and on. Even though the guy was starting to get on Joe's nerves too, I suspect he was keeping him around to at least mow the lawn, etc… as I recovered from knee surgery. Joe threw him out, finally, when the guy pawned some of his tools.

*****

CHAPTER FOUR

*"Let yourself be drawn by strange pull of what you
love-it will not lead you astray."-Rumi*

I again sense a closer relationship with him. He really does enjoy how well the paint job on the camper turned out. I'm thrilled he comes to events with me. He hands out compliments effortlessly about my artwork. "Maybe we'll even take a trip in it," he said.

We started talking about getting a dog. Sure enough, and *as if conjured up just for us,* he appeared free that week on Craigslist. So, it feels like a new kind of God note. It is very important for me to exercise. I'm on my third knee rebuild now. I need very strong leg muscles.

I have yet to find a *treadmill* that devotes itself to hovering around me whining until I use it. I needed this dog. I'm proud to walk my rough neighborhood with this fine and beautiful animal to protect me. Yet, it is also a lesson in patience for me. I can cuss and swear at every turn he annoys me on. "Fucker," I catch myself spewing at him. Wow. I'm appalled at *how much frozen rage is still inside of me.*

"Actually, I have a whole new understanding now of what your daughter must have suffered growing up." Joe said to me one day after witnessing such impatience.

(Alas, if relationship come along a little later in life and need some of the background filled in...with alternate methods... here's another purpose dogs can serve.)

*****

When Joe has reached a certain level of inebriation, he likes to go into deep conversations and press again about defining our relationship. Well, thankfully, I have been working my food addiction program pretty well these days. Somewhere in the promises, it states we will instinctively know what to say.

"I think that you like me just fine, but you want to reserve the right to play like you're *all that* if it can get you a rush."

"I love you," he blurted out. "You're my best friend."

But then he started a diatribe about sexual types and finding just the right one that he can control. I short circuited the conversation with a quick, "No one can control anyone." He acquiesced with a soft, "I know."

I went about some chore in another room, and we left it there. This was not a teachable moment. For example, food addicts like to think *they* are special. *They* want to believe they can eat like linebackers yet somehow have the body of a supermodel. So... not a *big jump* see other types of addicts getting *I am somehow so special* ideas in their heads.

He may be dreaming of some small tight bodied blonde who he would ride on top. Maybe he could just hold her by say, the torso, and maneuver her around like some sort of *inverse dildo*. Then, as long he's conjuring up the perfect woman, may as well throw in an uncanny appreciation for television viewing 24/7— also... *his* pick of the program.

*****

I've been working on my recovery for years, and it amazes me how many layers of pure shame are involved. I have yet even disclosed to Joe that I have weighed heavier than this at certain points in my life. I know what addiction is about. Food is *still* calling my name enough to keep me hovering *still* overweight. I'm too old and stretched out to compare with his perfect women, so it's not ever going to be me. But I don't really care.

Actually, I'm not the least bit interested in being someone's trophy girl, and I don't want to be a millionaire particularly either. But I do want to be respected for doing the best I can do with what I do have to work with. I need to also try to hold up my end of the bargain and actually do my part. Looking back on my upbringing, chances are that I was born a food addict...though it took me almost 50 years to realize it.

There is a solution for learning how to handle life on all of its terms without abusing food for my comfort, etc. And it is my job to try to be in recovery to the best of my ability. We are called to press in for the best life we can have… to *glorify God.*

Then alas! The tide turned. Even though he's still drinking, he has come to see me as an asset, at least. He's being very sweet to me. He caught up with me one night between our bedrooms for swooping kiss…*finally*! I kissed him right back too.

"I'm such an asshole," he muttered.

So, I too apologized for whatever my small transgression of the day had been.

He scoffs back with a "you don't do anything wrong." We kiss again and say the I love you's.

I peel away with "Good night." I *go into my room, and Joe … into his.* I believe that God does not want me to live in sin, and I have repented for this.

It was several days after this when I realized the "I'm such an asshole" may have been an apology for the past almost 2 years of total crap he just handed me.

He wants me to go out in public with him again now. One night he came along with me to an event at a very nice place. Joe suggested we go off by ourselves for a private dinner up ahead. It was another tender moment type conversation and a very enjoyable meal. He tells me in a very sincere and matter-of-fact way how he *loves* that I'm an artist. This isn't the first time through on this topic, but it ranges as a true appraisal.

I hope he also comes to understand and feels *honored* and noble enough to accept what is needed to produce art, mostly that I need to be allowed to voice what's coming through to *me*. I have to grasp what seems essential and arrange it in a way that shows it the most powerfully and significantly to me. And as long as I do it with honest sincerity, it will be worth *everything* as a miraculously rendered truth.

"No matter how slow the film, SPIRIT stands always still long enough for the photographer it has chosen." –Minor White

We continue to do more outings. At this point, *not to shame him for drinking* seems like the best approach to take, and let God deal with the rest. One night when he was tearing up, he told me he appreciates that I don't hold his alcoholism against him…that "that *I'm the only one* that hasn't."

When another person makes you suffer, it is because he suffers deeply within himself, and his suffering is spilling over, he does not need punishment: he needs help. -Thich Naht Hanh

I decided to just stay in the moment. No one could possibly be more fun to dance with. Picture lanky twisting legwork with a great big grin. Yeah, lots of moves. He roars out a laugh when I say we could be like peacocks where the male is more colorful. *Works for me…*

He tells me what a great person the lady who owns the bar is. She is a peppy, pretty, and petite ex-stewardess. I acknowledge that she seems nice. I know Joe's drinking moods well. It doesn't really take much before he's back to his resentments over his divorce. He misses his kids. Tears are shed. He goes there with anyone who will listen.

I have no doubt he fantasizes about this bartender gal here because she is peppy, pretty, and petite— not that I have anything against her for that really. I'm sad that he still gets so messed up over sex. But he's verbalized his feelings for me enough lately that I'm feeling pretty secure… though he did say he doesn't know *how* to love me. I don't know how to respond to this…especially since there's a possibility that *this is true on some level.*

Still, the bartender beauty makes some comment about how she'll end up with all the money he has on the bar before the nights over … with a knowing smile, of course. I file it away. I still default to fault-finding at times. But nowadays, I'm at least smart enough to *recognize it for what it is,* and even though I think it— Thank you, Jesus— I do not always speak it.

Yet, I'm still not sure what to do with these thoughts because I was really quite good at building a tremendous case against someone if I put my mind to to it. For Example: this chick is undoubtedly guilty of serving him well past the time that he should be cut off. *This fact alone could get brushed aside, however, as almost too cliché.* So, I fantasize the maximum trumped up level I could take this point to.

I remember many years ago I saw some documentary in the middle of the night where a good-looking guy was with a gal that had to weigh 5 or 6 hundred pounds. It seems like she was just wearing a sheet or something, and her body was taunt with the *mammoth*-ness of it…tits like watermelons. The guy would pour whole bottles of pure oil into her mouth, and she'd drink them down straight. "Feeders," they called the guy. Addiction and enabling were discussed, and I was repulsed.

Really, there must be some way I can show this bartender chick in that light. But I think that I am supposed to be learning not to push *anything*. My program does teach us to journal or make a phone call to stop obsessing, so here we are with that.

> *On this day I promised God and myself that I will let go of the problem which is destroying my peace of mind. I pray for detachment from the situation, but not from the suffering drinker who may be helped to sobriety through the change in my attitude and the love and compassion I am able to express."-One Day at a Time in Al-anon*

✶✶✶✶✶

He had spent the day drinking. It had again become almost round the clock. It was the night before Thanksgiving. Signs were up all-around town for extra DWI patrols. He was friendly to me on the phone earlier in the night, and I'd offered to come get him in an hour or so. But…I couldn't find him, so I went to bed. He called at two in the morning.

"Can I ask a favor?" he states, polite as hell. "Would you be so kind as to come get the dog? He's at the police station. The officer here is being decent enough to let me call you to come get him." He went on to tell me he thought he'd be locked up for at least a year.

I got the dog and as much information as possible. He got a DWI with other charges pending. The towing company said they'd taken his plates. The dog had eaten through a lot of important things inside this $500 vehicle. I paid the towing fee and let them have his rig. I felt big relief over it for sure. Five days later, he got out of jail. *He claims he's done drinking and that not having a vehicle is definitely a help with that.*

He has pursued trying to find an online job with unbelievable determination. Scam upon scam… upon scum. Yet he has held up with a positive attitude. He admits that the drinking has not been fun for a long time now. *Don't worry, he'd find some work.* He is nice to me all around.

He has now even signed the house over to me. All he asks is a room to stay in, he says. The love is coming through in some pretty neat ways.

Recently, we spent a nice evening at home watching a movie. Then he decided to take the dog out for a walk. I heard the front door close. *I figured I was safe to expel quite a gas build up. I let it rip with gusto.*

Oh no! I heard him snickering with *out and out* hilarity.

Dang! He and the dog were still in the front porch booting up. I didn't say a word… hoping *that* would allow his brain to try to conjure up any additional explanations for this type of noises. The next day, out of the blue, he decided to tell me a story about some old neighbors that would always "blow it *out their ass.*"

So okay, he knew exactly what it was. I'm going to chalk it up as a way for him to not feel so *less than* around me. I could tell him a great joke, but I sensed he'd get hung up on the word *married* in it… so… not worth telling him now…

"Why doesn't a women fart until after she's married?"

"She doesn't have an asshole until then."

*****

He went up north for Christmas with me. It was so perfect... nothing could have made my aging mother happier. As she sat playing Christmas music at the piano, she must have recognized my voice. She turned around in the small country church of my childhood on Christmas morning and saw us there...right behind her. *Surprise!* Great day.

But then, on the drive home, Joe got a big distancing plan going in his head again about some year-long *walk-a-thon*, and I just nodded along with it.

He did decide to go back for in-patient treatment... but still the same rinky-dink *don't hardly get through the first 3 steps program*... because he doesn't have insurance. He called me every day and told me he loved me. His *far-out plans* have tamed into practical thinking. He is very involved helping the program newcomers and friend to all. I am continuing to work a 12-step program... taking one day at a time.

This time around, I have more Al-anon programming under my belt. I am grateful that he is in my life. My recollections of the really painful things have become more diluted now. We are both working on ourselves.

I know that everything he tells me *in his God mode* comes from God, and *that alone* surpasses any other relationship I have known. His all-around natural born enthusiasm is such a gift. I see unlimited possibilities with God at the helm. He causes me to want to light *my* light when I can as well.

*****

Joe's been sober now more than 6 months and still going to weekly meetings that he takes part in. I go and help set up chairs, etc., as well. Then, one night after the meeting, Joe told me *a lady at the meeting gave him some shit about what a nice car I drive.*

Well, since his painting business is really taking off, he was able to manipulate me into signing off on a truck for him again too. God will do as He sees fit about that. Anyway, Joe started acting like he didn't need me the second he got wheels of his own again.

I've researched the *"got sober… then what"* literature enough to know *most couples don't make it through this.* Thankfully though, I believe my Higher Power understanding… has reached a new level. God does have my best interest at heart, and it *will* work out the way it's supposed to. I don't need to try to push or prod anything. I don't need to try to reason or defend or persuade. I just need to do what I need to do… to have my own serenity on a daily basis.

His child support issues from his teen years has come home to roost. He's not going to have decent credit *ever* unless he absolutely buckles down and manages to get into some kind of plan with payments or whatever. And… suffice it to say, I've cajoled along those lines enough already.

Then also, what to do about sex? I detour from going there even in a conversation with him. I want to be in God's will. Yet the level of porn I've been consuming lately is getting pretty disgusting, which I am sure is not in God's will either— *so where does that leave me?* I wonder if I'm using that as a cover for the things I don't want to see in myself because then I don't have to admit that Joe's basically just not into me. On and on those thoughts go.

Also, now I've noticed that when I'm just trying to sketch in significant background details, Joe really gets impatient with my *how-something —went-down* style of relaying the day-to-day stuff. I want to take offense at this because I see how it highlights the finished viewpoint. I believe myself to be rather good at it. In fact, anyone who's been exposed to it really should trust that such a thing is wondrous and *appreciate* it. But then, as he says, he just has no patience anymore at all. We are both living in deprivation to some extent, I know.

Lately, too, I've seen the word *limitations* in a new light… actually, in what I think may be the light he perhaps sees me in too much. I think that he's been through a string of women, porn, and prostitutes… and that sexy *little* cuties hold a place of great desire in his head.

Yet, why would I not want to present myself in my best light… the type of beauty that is a *joy* to behold? Feminine can be so sweet, why deprive a person from a *pleasure* that may be a possibility? It is a treat.

"Just for today, I will be agreeable. I will look as well as I can, dress becomingly, talk low, act courteously, criticize not one bit, not find fault with anything, and not try to improve or regulate anybody except myself."

*****

Maybe I can only safely be in a relationship with another recovering food addict? But I am also an artist, and in that realm, *safe* is not *always* a good word. Plus, when I do try to picture what eating a good meal *in a good way* looks like, his modeling fits that pretty well. Do I see the cups as half full here? I want to. I want to be *that* girl.

I can *try* to be more relationship friendly myself. I never give him credit for all the little things he does. He follows the news stories, and he tries to keep me up on the stuff I should know. He brings home containers I can use to separate out my paint supplies in. He brought home a room divider thing… *he thought I could do something neat with.* One day, Joe even handed me a bag of old bobby pins saying, *"art project?"*

But I heard him tell someone last week that *he figures he'll die a lonely old man.* My heart aches over his self-appointed epithet… to be remembered as the man who *couldn't quite find the love he needed.* I want to help his hurting, but he has no intention of letting me in that way… right now. It is indeed one step forward, two steps back… and yet we continue.

We could have it all, *I think,* if we would just get past the emotional damage going on here. Believe me, he can resist adopting someone else's mindset—at least as well as anything else he does. He is stubborn. I pray that he begins to see that *when sexuality is based on love rather than physical looks, sex lives will not be diminished by inevitable physical changes.* I will pray that *we do not get lost in our own pasts of domestic strife and hardships…AND …I pray that I am not stuck in some dangerous state of nostalgia with him.*

*****

This morning, as I was putting on my makeup, I caught myself conjuring up a dialogue suggesting the *foreplay* concept should also transcend into other areas like conversations about home improvement projects or what to watch on television. You know like finding a fun and pleasurable way to *work into those things too*. Wouldn't that be awesome?

But then I wonder if I may be trying to *control an outcome* with this thought process. Then I think it is ok to know what your ideas really are. I remember a line I read in some book about *piss-ass unarticulated unhappiness* as *not* a good thing. I'm pretty sure because it ties into boundary issues. That's a big area for addicts to work on. But…I also want to be ready for the moment God tells me to lay some idea out there.

Merry-go-round mind… *again*. Then my disease kicks in, and I overeat, so I don't have to think about anything except the misery of that. I ate so much this afternoon. I am now thinking Al-anon is probably something to learn for *real*. I did call around until I got a new sponsor for overeating, at least. Dear God in heaven, help me help *myself*.

I see a column in the paper talking about how people get caught up in *thriller* movies. It's an adrenaline rush for people to hover in a state of baited breath over w*hat in the world is going to happen* when the story gets going into the really scary stuff. *Really, should they even go down those stairs?* So, of course, I see that as an open invitation on keep right on laying out the gory details for *this* category. It is a tense terrain, but I'm feeling called to the deep work through it.

So… one Saturday, we drove 5 hours each way… to attend Joe's company picnic. A few miles shy of getting there, we managed an *almost intimate little chat*. He'd been going on about his Dad's many defects and offenses. I steered the conversation over to reiterate what his dad told me… he'd been impotent since he married his last wife. Joe went on to bring up several almost *stereotypical dirty old man* indiscretions that had also been chalked up to his dad since then. I rolled out some ditty like, "Maybe they think that *young voluptuousness* will somehow help them get it up."

Joe did such a sweet and automatic, *no way*… I treasure it to this day. Who knows why he said it. *Maybe* to make me think he still finds me attractive.

From there though, he went into his *all too common* distancing with me "I don't want to sit down" responses to friendliness on my part at the picnic.

I do feel that Joe has limited insight into the concept of tolerance and *not* taking other people's inventory. It is very hard for him not to criticize. At least we were almost back before he lit into his sharpest attack of the day… about my driving. Still, I know I *can't* let loose with a scathing *maybe if you'd get your license* because it would be as shame producing as anything that I could have hit him with …when he was drinking. I am barely holding on.

I had a meltdown the next day, trying to program a new scanner for his business. It was a bitch from hell to set up. Then, he told his boss over the phone the reason he couldn't send pictures was because the scanner wasn't up. I tried to explain they could go out in e-mail. Joe went off on me. He had some little white lie planned to say to him, *and if he heard what I said,* this would reveal his twist. He continued to *full scale rant* at me. I say nothing.

I was suddenly very aware of *what* my daughter has always tried to tell me. She'd say that when you're criticized to such an extent, it really is hard to believe that you're loved. Sadly, the *ranter* is not capable of love at this point. But wow, my heart just goes out to my daughter for how I must have made her feel. And I do love her. When he is again decent the next morning, I know he is *trying not to blow it.*

*****

We *did* get the camper out and make it up north. I figured it would be tense. But I felt like *just to do it* would *establish a little less fear* for the next time. Unfortunately for me, he still sees *spontaneous* as a really good thing. I go more with an AA idiom of it where it is considered just another version of *self-will run riot.* Because believe me… the one on the other end of it has to waste a lot of time waiting *when there is no plan in place.*

It also seemed like he was worried that I may have some expectations of intimacy. Well, two can play that game. He and the dog slept in the tent just like we said, and no other possible version ever came up. But, jeez… we live in the same house together already so I mean *really*… sometimes I can't even imagine the level of his insecurities. All in all, the trip wasn't *too* bad... he loves the camper's appeal, and he gushes all the credit for it... *to me.*

He can campfire cook better than anyone I know. I had moments of almost screaming fun on the boat. *Go faster!* But mostly... he has got to stop the criticizing. Talk about *talking* all the fun out of things. I was a little sad when we went back to the club house where his son had his wedding dance a few years back. That was such a great night. Joe danced and kissed and hugged and loved on me so sweetly; it is forever etched into me. This time, there's nothing. But expectations are resentments waiting to happen. Life goes on.

We had a big blow-out fight on the third day. I kept it to a basic point about his disrespect for my time. This is an area I need to set boundaries in with him anyway, so I took the fight there instead of going with *his* lead-in "I don't own him" drama he was puffin' up and giving me.

*****

We've been back from that almost a week, and I need to get it together. Tonight, when he supposedly went to an AA meeting, I had to run out for a binge of peanuts and raisins. As the dog was *leering* out the car window, it reminded me of a look Joe has sometimes when we're driving down the street. He's does full scale commentaries on women's asses: *look at that one, Jesus, cheeks just a floppin' thinkin' they're all that...*

I remember the wonderful comfort level *with my previous boyfriend* when naked. I think there's a good chance Joe has never been able to have comfort like this because he is so critical. Who would dare to *really bare* in any way? But I still ate over this stupid shit, and it has got to stop. I spent time thinking maybe he's *not the one.*

I want more music in my life for starters, and the list goes on. But then, I read where the Mom tries to teach her daughter how tension makes a relationship worth more. Plus, I hear the song "Heavenly Days" somewhere, and I *know* that's what got me through the worst of his drinking last year. Honestly, he'd go off on me so hard over the least little thing, but later, he'd tell me I did exactly the right thing by just walking away.

48

Then, I remember that my theme song this year is about *wanting to make it work.* Even when he's absolutely crazy, it comes down to learning how to navigate a safe path-way around what truly is a mental illness, *or* get out altogether. Since I can't afford it and neither can he, we both have to play our cards very carefully. We are being forced to practice patience and tolerance... what a set-up.

Sometimes though, I fill with hate and loathing. I feel used and abused. He is about 8 months sober now. He wouldn't come with me to the art car parade last night. So, I took a girlfriend, and it was really fun. I'm sad that Joe and I inhibit each other as much as we do these days, and I wonder how to *fix* that.

The central air conditioner is a major bone of contention. I am sure that somehow my bedroom doesn't have the right setup to return air or something. I can feel clouds of hot air just hovering. I am in hot flash land besides. Try as I might to deal with this issue enough to at least get *some* sleep, he continues to go total control freak over it. I pay the utility bills. I do not rant about his leaving the light on all night to see his truck. I have kindly suggested he grab an extra blanket. All to no avail. I am sick of not getting good sleep, and I am sick of being so disrespected.

But I also know that recurrent senseless raging is self-destructive behavior. I know I cannot continue to have them even *if they are justified* because they stop spiritual and emotional growth. I think I need to get back in touch with my sponsor to get a better plan.

I have to learn to deal with my negative emotions. I spend the bulk of some days unconsciously pulling the circles on the necklace he gave me so hard that I can't believe it hasn't broken by now. Finally, I go buy a window air conditioner to put in my room... even though it is more expensive to run than our central air conditioning unit.

Anger may be a natural reaction to frustrating situations, but does it pave the way for calm and reasonable communication? I spend the morning over-eating. Again, I beg, "Help me, Jesus. Show me the right plan for abstinence. Thank you."

Since the incident up North when he made the *I don't own him* stink, he's doing things without me that we had been doing together, like visiting his Dad. Then suddenly, he did invite me to do it one night last week but decided later that he was too tired, and we didn't go. Who knows? Maybe he is bi-polar. Hopefully, he is at least working through his *family of origin* issues that, sooner or later, we all should do.

He casually mentions to me that tomorrow night he is taking his sister and his step Mom to the casino for supper. No mention of inviting me. My feelings were hurt, but I didn't show it. He goes without me for any number of reasons, none of which are good ones in my mind. But God is big. There's no telling what could develop. I could end up being so gracious about his fucking bullshit that he eventually does want to take me to these things.

*****

So, I finally come across information about "sexual anorexia." This seems to be a significant area to understand as far as this relationship goes. The book I ordered should be here next week. I did calmly let him know that his *jumping into overriding things… so fast…* makes me feel like I can hardly have a conversation with him. The look he gave me was real relationship mull. It had an afterglow to it. I think he was listening.

Al-anon-asked us to learn to distinguish between saying disagreeable, critical things vs. statements that shed valuable light on a situation, *without hurting feelings*. Newly sober alcoholics are so braced for rejection; they imagine things that aren't intended. Acting out may be the only recourse they know at this point.

Can I make a difference with God's help? I really will have to learn patience, tolerance, love, and goodwill. I also realize that *the one who first sees the attitude needed for change* has the obligation to model it in a relationship.

Wow… he did now invite me to go to the Casino. I met him there when I got off work. He is wonderful to me that whole day. The Casino floor was *uneven* in a spot, and he had to do a fast shuffle to stay upright. He started to giggle about it. Then, we both broke out laughing in *total abandon*. . It warmed my heart to enjoy him so much again.

*****

Now I *have* read the Dr. Carnes' book explaining sexual self- hatred. I took a lot of notes too. Many, many insights to work with here. This book shows how sexual intimacy *is an opening* for possible betrayal… in *damaged* people's minds.

Thus, the whole barrier thing gets set up, which eventually doesn't work. Emptiness and anxiety come back. *And note to self: where there is deprivation, an addictive behavior will present itself somewhere else.*

We were doing so great at the on-set; I hadn't been able to figure out how it could get so messed up so fast. But, *aha* moments did abound as I read this book. Healing usually requires an environment of nurturing safety. Good thing a life of service is a significant factor in what recovery's about. Maybe I do need to drop the whole *what about me thinking*, or at least find the middle ground.

Plus, creativity involves at least examining our beliefs, even if we don't necessarily change them. In fact, much of art is about exaggerating the littleness in life that need to be brought into a sharper focus to get re-examined.

When I catch myself thinking there's no way Joe is ever going to jump all the hoops that seem to be required, I remind myself how powerful God is. But since Joe does not want to come clean on his long over-due child support debt, I can't imagine what his *motivator* would ever be.

Joe's brother died only a short time ago. Then, on the day of *that* funeral, his step Mom weakened with her cancer to a point of soon to be dead as well. Joe has been all business, handling the incredibly involved details. Also, during all this extended family time, he may be building a new relationship with at least one of his three legitimate kids.

During the time around that funeral, one of his sisters and her boyfriend stayed with us a few days too. This is my favorite of all his siblings.

Joe was really decent to me the whole time they stayed with us. I felt the love, even though, of course, it was in no way overt. But then, the distancing that always comes behind his letting me in a little bit.

This time my offense was suggesting a more efficient bill payment method to save me at least a half hour trip to the bank for money orders. He wouldn't hear of it *because we had already discussed the plan.* Considering I knew he was still smarting over family matters that didn't go the way he had planned, it was stupid for me to say anything. But I did. By the time I suggested the part where *it would save a half hour of my time,* he snapped.

Days and days of "*Oh, I wouldn't want to waste your precious time…*" alternated with totally ignoring me. In the first round of this, I did try to get across my point— that the word *discuss* means at least two people get to have input. He said I made that point loud and clear. I hope so, but I kind of doubt it.

During the actual screaming match itself, he made some wild remark, like *his name's going back on everything pretty soon.*

To which I replied, "Happy, happy day." I am tired of his suggesting I am here to *exploit.* I'm sure just because he's throwing tons of money on his daughter now, he's hoping she'll sign on anything he asks.

Plus, he wants his daughter to come for long and frequent visits. This would be much easier at this two-bedroom house *if I wasn't here.* And finally, he's starting to make such good money. Doesn't he *deserve* arm candy, especially since he's been living in such a deprived state? Have I mentioned yet that I do have paranoia? I do.

*****

CHAPTER FIVE

*"If you are irritated by every rub,
how will your mirror be polished?"* —*Rumi*

Addicts are extremists. Joe's fear of even the slightest slight gets him in a total rejection mode. But I still have to create appropriate boundaries for my life if I want to experience transformation. Well, *hallelujah*, I just realized that if I don't even care that he goes off somewhere without me, he will not find it all that much fun to do. Plus, I just read *"less said, sooner mended"* in my daily al-anon reading.

We hardly have a clue anymore how to communicate in a way that works well, how to really understand what's going on with each other, mood by mood, and situation by situation. But the type of person I'd like to become *does* have these skills, so it is up to me to start acting with that integrity now.

For me, it means I need to get fit and healthy, and I need to write and publish. I cannot be spending time obsessing about what he is or is not doing. I need to expand my own capacity to love. Committing to change is an act of faith. I *need* to have faith that I will succeed and that I will be OK. This is what I must do!

"Two consciousness, each dedicated to personal evolution, can provide an extraordinary stimulus and challenge to one another, and ecstasy can become a way of life." –Dr. Patrick Carnes.

He is right. I'm sure *conflict* and *honesty* are an invitation to greater intimacy, and successful partnering is about two people who are really able to see that the problems lie in themselves.

Dr. Carnes' book also reports that *addicts commonly act out dramatically outside of a committed relationship but are usually compulsively non-sexual within that relationship* certainly made me think of Joe. I pray that, at some point, he will be interested in coming with me to some kind of recovery group. Yet, my sexual intimacy problems are on me. Why do I still feel so flawed that

I don't take the weight off?

Avoidance addicts had childhoods where no one was there to relieve their pains. They don't understand that *a relationship can relieve abandonment experiences.* No one fits perfectly in any category, and everything is on a continuum, but my guess is this played significantly into his failed marriage. I know my incest issue, together with shame and then the weight issue, was a big factor in my unsuccessful marriage.

This is very interesting stuff. So many are drawn toward relationships but cannot fully commit because on some deep level, they think they are avoiding the chance they will be abandoned. I have to say that my favorite one liner in the whole book was *"self- actualized people are not threatened by strangeness; rather they are intrigued by it."*

✶✶✶✶✶

Well, evidently, I must not be very self-actualized yet. ANOTHER big fight ensues. He was smoking a cigarette, so I turned the air purifier on. This is exactly what I bought it for. He turned it off. The argument got nasty fast. His new line lately— "I am the dictator here"— was the last straw. I have felt too much disrespect. I let go with a big stick.

"I'd think twice before I'd drive that truck again if I were you," I say to him, even though I'd warned myself time and time again not to go there.

Then, the whole *are you threatening me* thing from him. "Get the fuck out of my house," he says.

"You don't tell me what to do. I'm sick of you. Your shit's just getting so old." On and on, I go yelling… not in compliance once again with the calm approach program. The *no stopping* thing you know…till I finally just have to go to bed …to stop myself from keeping it going.

The next morning, I pray for right words and tell him, *"I'll go, but not for two years."* This is the amount of time I need to get my credit ready for a different house. I hear him moan on that note. "That should give you enough time to clean up your child support bill and get yourself financially able to sign back on the house. Why should you care anyway? You're not even in a position to be in an appropriate intimate relationship with anyone with such a credit issue hanging over your head. It's been this giant looming over you most of your life that you're too afraid to slay."

He says nothing.

I meter out to him that "I've just had it with the disrespect. I'm done trying. I do love you on some deep level, but I really don't think this relationship will ever work *without* some help." He was quiet for a little while, but then we just changed the subject. There comes a point where analysis becomes overdone.

I've even caught myself fantasizing that someday if we ever even go out to eat again, I could role play this point home to him. There's a warp in my brain that's ready with a lovely little skit to perform for him when he gets around to mentioning, as he inevitably does, how I am n*ot his girlfriend…* to me or *anyone that he even remotely feels may wonder.* As soon he hands me the now almost predictable comment in that area, here's what I see transpiring: I could just quietly rise up out of my chair with a sweet, sweet smile. From there, I could gracefully walk over to a surrounding table and engage in polite conversation with these people.

Hello, how are you? How's the meal? Good. That's great. Say, by the way, in case you were wondering, I'm not his girlfriend. Didn't want you to get the wrong idea is all. Ok well then nice meeting you! Cheerio!

Maybe even approach another table… just to make *double sure* no one thought such a thing. In my dreams, a laugh like this will teach him.

There is dignity in admitting our wounds. This is the first step in healing them. I am happy to come to this thinking here. Thoughts do matter. They create our emotions, which, in turn, create our reality. When we let go of past negativity, we can create our future from a different frame of reference.

Finally, too, I have been able to distinguish how this is different from just storing up grievances, indignities, and records of oppressions that can pretty much accidentally restore them all the way back to their painful realities. This is not a memorandum about horrors endured. My task is to watch for my own faults and root them out.

Yes, there have been days when I have hated his twisted heart, but I cannot *make* anything happen. I need to let *this* come to me and do the best I can with what I've got. I am diligently reviewing literature for setting good boundaries. I do understand how the caretaker role can damage boundaries both ways. I get that I do.

I asked Joe if he wanted to take a long cigarette butt… he had left in the ashtray with him…as he headed out one morning. He *called me out* as some sort of offensive *caretaker*. He could not have been more wrong. *I just didn't want to smell it all day*, and I had already experienced full-scale attack for throwing such *treasures* away.

He turned my motive for running it out to him into some chore I performed that can *have the potential to cause resentment*, I think. I'm pretty sure he does have some working knowledge of these concepts. But I *wasn't* trying to be nice. It was a self-protection move that was only costing me a trip to the front porch. I let it go. No point. In fact, I sometimes think the biggest problem in his childhood may have been that no one curtailed his temper tantrums. *Period.*

As I was setting up the laptop again in the basement, I see that he whipped the extension cord over into a pile of boxes in the corner. I am tempted to approach this with gentle "now was that really hurting you?" But if his upbringing skipped tolerance for the rights of others and it comes from me now, is this classifying me in a *Mommy role?*

Sometimes that may be true, but I am an addict myself. So, I still have enough dysfunctional attitudes in areas like *confidence on the job,* etc. where *he steps in* and, at least, attempts to teach me the skills. I am still considering the possibility that we can learn to graciously fill in each other deficits.

He is making efforts to be closer again. He went shopping when I was at work last Sunday. He even called to see if I needed anything. He was very pleasant. Oh so excited to show me his new clothes and shoes that night. "Oh," he says, "and I did something else today too."

"What's that?"

"I got a full body message."

Not knowing what to say, I cover with a trite, "Oh, where?"

"Some nice Asian place. It was really good."

I'm remembering that I got some great massages a few years back at the chiropractor's office. I mostly thought how nice sex with Joe would be throughout each session. I bought him a gift certificate. He never used it. "It would seem too sexual… I'd be embarrassed," he stated, though I assured him this gal was matronly.

Anyway, I didn't keep the conversation going about it. I kind of think he may have gotten turned on to the point where he did want me? But history tells me this mood won't last all that long.

*****

Joe did *not* invite me to his Dad's facility's function coming up. Since we got back from camping in July and it now October, I have not been out there except on the day of his brother's funeral. Then, on top that, his phone rang with a *special ring tone*, and he *did not* answer it.

So, *what about* the whole sexual anorexia issue where they have to be loved into healing? *Who is ever going to put up with this degree of shit long enough to actually do it?* How many Anne Sullivan's are there in this world? And how conceited was that statement? Joe is a pain, but is he equivalent to Helen Keller? I'm thinking of Rosa Parks now.

Supposedly, I have learned that support usually works best when both people understand that healing is a *process*. And a very basic principle is simply not to put others in a position where making the pile of crow they have to eat *even bigger*. Translated, I think that means there's no real value in putting them on defense.

So… he left around 11 am, mumbling something about going to visit his Dad. He came back home around 6 pm. I was working on something in the basement at the time. I did not rush up to see him. Later, I just washed up and went to bed.

The next morning, he initiated friendly conversation, so I listened as he told about his frustration with his family. He went on to say his dad called him the night before and that he had just let it ring. I suspect he tells me this in case I thought it was someone else, to put my mind at rest. He went on to say that he decided to just call up a guy friend from the treatment center to spend time with him. They went to a movie.

But then he called up some gal, the next night, for almost an hour chit chat about interior decorating projects and maybe incorporating them into his painting business. I went to bed. Still, I could hear a lot of his laughing and lines. *I'm a Christian you know* struck pretty close to the bone.

I got the impression a few days later that he suspected *I was up to something* by going to the health club early in the mornings. "I don't say a word." He says, "I just observe."

I let him off his hook. "I can get *you* a really cheap membership at my health club, you know."

Calmness for a day or so, then things started to tense up again. A lot was involved to get the paperwork figured out for several weeks' worth of payroll and collecting on multiple jobs. As I head out to go to the health club, I cheerfully ask him to write down what he needed me to get out of the bank… for payroll. He said nothing. Since there was no note when I got back, I called him.

He huffs at me about how I am *harping* on him. "This is bordering on harassment."

I heard myself trying to calm him down with even a stray *honey* thrown in there somewhere, which was scary to me. But *blah, blah, blah* on he goes. I managed to not hang up. He wraps it up. I move on with my day. A couple hours later, he calls and actually apologizes. Interestingly enough, I *did* feel better instantly. All was forgiven. *Nice.*

I still wonder if this is really meant to be. I have lined the evidence up against alcoholism, bi-polar, bi-sexual, and borderline personality disorder. I review my new knowledge of the whole sexual anorexia issue too. I see that this is a major component here to deal with. Love and nurturing is the solution for that, but it feels like we've just been through so much bullshit.

Last week, he went to collect somewhere in the neighborhood of $3500's from one of the contractors he works for. He called to say that the guy was questioning the bill to such a degree that I should provide cold hard evidence for him. I drop what I am doing and scramble to look for what I can find to help support this billing. He leads into this call by the way with *"if you're looking for something to do."*

I am *never* looking for something to do. I am always trying to find the time to do things I *like* to do. So, I am *not* happy about this request, especially since it has been an ongoing hassle to get him to organize paperwork I need in a way that is efficient. This is a not a job I have asked for, but his business is really taking off, and I want him to succeed.

Moreover, I am also the signer on the business checking account, so at least the banking *has* to be on me. He typically waits until the last minute to bring the needed paperwork around and then expects me to figure out the billing in the way *they* are asking for it. I have nicely explained the format I need him to submit it to me many times, but *no way…*

It is also typically past my bedtime when he finally gets started on the basic lay-out for me. Then just to set the stage for torture all around… he has the TV on with *how to kill the person you live with* programs… fills the air with toxic carcinogens and turns up the heat.

This night now and about this $3500 bill. I cannot figure out where the problem really lies because it is a misunderstanding about billings that are 4 weeks back, much of the paperwork is in his truck, and we have yet to lock into a good system with this contractor to document accounts paid, etc. Joe calls about a half dozen times to get me try and figure it this way and that way, *all of which I have already done*, but I am unable to get a true picture, and I cannot believe that he has not come home to help me.

He is visiting his bedridden Dad, but this is something that he does daily and more than once a day some days. When he does finally get home, I have not been able to produce the evidence needed, and he starts to *lay the blame on me* about what could be the loss of around a thousand dollars.

I am not willing to tolerate this belligerence. By the time he throws in "I pay you to do the bookkeeping," I have had it. He has no real idea how much time is involved and makes cracks about how he over pays me to boot. *He pushed too far.*

I went off hard core, listing everything I just mentioned. He sat in *my* recliner, that he's completely overtaken, barking off "fuck you, get outta my house. Get the fuck out of my house."

I go straight to the bonus round. *"Fuck you, it's not your house, and I dare you to get in your truck tomorrow and try to drive it. All I have to do is call 911 to pick you up, and you sit in jail for a fuck of a long time… out of my hair. Your shit is over."* I am right in front of him now as he still sits in the recliner. My fists are clenched, and I am even *swinging* at him.

I see the look in his eyes, registering how really seriously bad this is getting. He did catch my fists at every swing in and just closed them gently, by the way, but I still had enough wiggle room to pull my hand back out and attempt to throw more jabs. *"Plus, by God, you had enough time to sit in the VFW playing pull-tabs last Saturday when you knew I needed help figuring this stuff out."*

"Oh, waa, waa. Just because you don't have a life."

"And then you can't even come home tonight to help with this when you *know* the bookwork has to get *completely* figured out." I keep trying to throw a swing in, and it has gotten to be like its choreographed. I added in his latest crime while I was at it.

"And don't you *dare* throw my washcloth out again. I need that to hold the water in for a bath." I accent the syllables to coordinate with my continued attempts swinging at him.

He does a come-back, "Why don't you just go buy a goddamn plug for it?"

Well, he was drinking during the time we were trying to get this house *livable,* so consequently, the tub and shower install is less than stellar. The internal mechanism to plug the water does not drop down. I have to put a thick washcloth over the drain screen to hold the water in if I want to take a bath. Several times recently, I have come home to find it thrown out on the hallway floor.

It is possible that since he prefers showers, he has forgotten what is actually involved with the current set-up. However, at what point—can he please, Dear God— become adult enough to have a conversation vs. having fits and throwing things like a fucking three-year-old? (Like I just did.)

Because the tub drain screen is permanently attached, this plug thing he is suggesting is *not* a possibility. Yet, even in my rage, I am aware that I should still not intentionally shame him about this fucked up set-up he has imposed.

In fact, even the threat to let him go to jail for driving without a license, I have carefully calculated numerous times. I see how it could very easily add up to be the last straw because *if, in fact, my job here is to provide the nurturing, trusting relationship he's never known,* THIS could very well be the total end of that.

But here I go, doing it anyway. Is my shortcoming acting up, or is my Higher Power instinctively guiding my boundary setting?

"Oh, so now you're going to steal my house?"

"It's in my name… you still owe me as much as you put in it, and I do the bulk of the daily work around here." This line I deliver with a fairly calm tone.

I take my leave. I go lay on my bed. I hear him saying something I can't make out. I see my chest rising up and down like a hem-i engine. I curse out a string of *"fuck off, fuck off, fuck off!"*

I decided that, as long as we are doing this, I may as well keep at it. I go back out there, and he is sitting in front of the computer. I rush up to him with a new round of accusations. When he was just in treatment this last time, *every day,* his phone calls to me ended with "I love you."

I knew that this was not exactly a sign of *all is well* because I was still being introduced as his best friend vs. girlfriend. But still, *even this* has completely gone away with the addition of him having his own wheels, *illegally and on my back.* And try as he might, I know he will not be able to point to any single event to justify some behavior of mine… causing the end of even hearing that now. So…. again… I get right in his face, "besides that… *you fucking low-life,* all you do is use people. Every day in treatment, every phone call was, *I love you, I love you.* You just fucking USE people."

I see then … that he has been looking up real estate quit claims on the computer. He tells me that he's calling his daughter and *putting the house in her name.*

"Call her all you want. I'm not going to sign anything. I'm not the one *going scrambling* here. I'm not the one trying to play dictator."

Then, he goes to stir something he's been cooking *for days* in the crock pot and states in a cold collected tone, "Oh, I ain't gonna be the one scrambing."

I've said my piece, so I just go back to bed and try to comprehend the fallout. *Wow.*

*****

I had read the books Al-Anon puts out about how tricky sobriety can be, especially the first year. They contend that the re-establishment of a satisfactory relationship may be brought forth if both partners are willing to contribute patience, loyalty, respect, and honesty. So, chances are I have really blown it.

Theoretically, the alcoholic's hidden guilt is at the core of their explosive accusations; the rage is really at themselves but vented at the nearest person. My job is to come to recognize these behaviors for what they are and not take them personally. *I can't imagine how bad it gets for the people that haven't read these books.*

Suddenly my bedroom door flies open, and he tells me to move my camper from the back lot off of the alley so he can put his truck up there on blocks. Far be it for me to stand in the way of him actually doing the right thing. I rush up there in slippers with a jacket over my nightgown and move it to the street. I come in and go back to my bed. As I lay there, I feel mostly numb, but I'm hoping I'll at least get a little bit of sleep.

The next morning at my usual 4:45am, I make coffee and an omelet. I watch Joyce Meyers on TV while I eat. When I go to my room, he gets up. I take my time getting dressed and putting on my make-up. I go down to the basement to do the daily homework for my 12 step program. I come back up, make my lunch, take my vitamins, grab my workout bag, and head out for the day. We did not speak. He's reading the paper, but his look comes off flushed. I am glad to have the time to hit the fitness club before work.

Somewhere around 8:30 am, I check my e-mails. The contractor who had balked about the billing the night before had sent an apology. We were right on. I forward these e-mails to Joe. When I have a chance to call him later about it, *he is wonderful to me.*

"Wow, last night was really bad. We're both a couple of hotheads who probably shouldn't be in the same room together when we're mad. I apologize."

Again, *instantly*, I do feel forgiveness. "Thanks, I say, it does make a difference when you apologize. I appreciate it." Then he promises Friday night will be paperwork night from now on.

Wednesday morning, I drove the camper to work and then put it back in its spot when I got home because, of course, there is no truck there... up on blocks. Thursday morning, I tried for easy going chit-chat when I was getting ready for work. "I did manage to get that bike rack on the camper yesterday. It fits really well."

"Oh, that's good. Say, where's the generator these days? I haven't seen it around lately."

"It's over by the furnace. Why?"

"No reason. I just haven't seen it lately, and I like to keep track of things."

This rings a little false with me, but I attempt normalcy with a "Have a good day."

I spend the day obsessing about this remark. I come to believe that the only possible reason he would have for trying to remember where we put the generator is because he has already divvied up our property in his head. I know both sides of his personality well enough to know that, in a certain mood, he could very easily just put a crew of his guys on packing me up, changing the locks, and moving me out.

What really scares me is that if he does this, I will *have* to get the cops involved, prove my name is the only name on the deed, and get a restraining order against him. *This* then will become the thing that will be unforgivable and take him down.

He was tied up late at work, but in a good mood when he did get home that night. Then by the time Friday rolled around, he was pretty efficient with what I needed for figures to get the cash payroll together for his crew. I finagled a way to get to the bank on my work time to accomplish this and picked up a Taco Salad on my way back. I just got done eating when he called. I had already decided to take the rest of the day off because it was a 3 day weekend, and I wanted to get a jump on my errands so I could work on my writing.

I tell him I'm coming home and that I'll call when I get there with the payroll cash. At that time, he invited me to meet him for lunch. I recognized this as an appeasement, so I accepted. I decided that somehow my food program will survive his inability to plan more than minutes ahead of time and that it is worth it to acknowledge his effort. The pleasantries throughout the meal are somewhat stilted. He talks about some business lunch he had recently where he has been invited to get some free hotel room for the night near the big Christmas party his boss is throwing.

He does *not* invite me to come with him. I once again feel like the brunt of the whole *throw me a bone.* I say nothing. He then takes up the topic of his Dad.

"I'd like to go visit him sometime."

"You should. He'd love it."

"I'm not going there without you. That's dumb."

"Why?"

"I don't know how to respond to the issues he brings up when he gets me alone."

"Well, I think it would be good to know what his issues are."

"His issues are that he doesn't think I had fun on vacation with you, etc."

As I watch Joe's expression change, I am able to see all of his composure melt away into a small wrinkled chin. I hurt for him. I decide that's enough jab for now. I know enough about addiction to know the disease is responsible for blind spots. They serve the purpose of helping the individual be able to live with themselves, so I really should accept it. Yet, I can't tell you how many times he has pointed out to me *the games his dad plays*. So, I *do* still find it baffling that he doesn't realize how transparent his game playing is.

Last year, we did up all the paperwork and signed the house over to me to save it from his secret big child support bill. I let him do his story to his dad about how he's *added* my name on the house because (as he grabs my hand) "we're in love." This is now something like the third round of that scenario, by the way.

Saturday night, we very comfortably watched a movie together on TV. Today is now Sunday. I have decided to tidy up some boundaries as long as we are still in the shell-shock aftermath stage of the big showdown that previous Monday night. I nicely asked *if we were going to work on his billing paper-work.*

He answered with a crabby "Can you let me wake up?"

At least I am able to later use *that* as a point of reference about the double standard going on here… .because if *I'm tired, too bad.* I go downstairs and work on my projects, *thinking I did OK* because my purpose was to alert him to the agenda. When I went up later, I see that he was working on the billings. I join him. When we got to the part where I asked him what he thought I should get paid this month, it got a little snippy. So, I told him I'd do his bookkeeping on a time card by the hour, and he does all the prep work the way I asked for it.

Then, I touch on the child support issue with a concerning tone. *Every day, he puts himself in the position of being jailed for driving without a license. It's scary. Why would he want to subject himself to that?* Plus, I mention that even though he hates me… remember he still needs me to do his banking. *Is his daughter going to drive 5 hours …one way…every week to withdraw the cash payrolls, etc.?*

In response, he told me my problem was that *I needed to get laid.*

I said that I'd have *no problem in that area should I choose to partake.*

He threw in a line about *no wonder my daughter doesn't come around; I'm such a bitch.*

I come back with *no filters.* "She doesn't come around because she can't *stand* you, and she's really sad that I live here."

He is very quiet for a while, and I am *so* surprised with what he says next. He cocks his head to the side and pauses before he says, "That's not really true."

"It is." I am instantly troubled by the *bridge burning caliber* of this too. Plus, is he somehow suggesting that *very little* of what we punch each other with… *we really mean?*

I go for another direct hit. "So, answer me this… when we met and you said you were looking for someone to go to church with and bike etc… for a balanced life… *were you just plain lying?* Is it just some kind of line you use?"

"My life is balanced. I like it just fine. So now… you're going to judge me?"

"I'm not judging you. I'm just trying to dig myself out of my own hole, work my own program, and avoid making that mistake again."

From there, we moved into how fucking *noble* he is to let me live here… *blah, blah, blah.* "Why *do* you live here?"

"I've asked myself that many times, and it just seems like I'm supposed to be here."

Joe throws out some lines about how *he was just trying to help me out with a place to live. I'm like every other woman he's ever known…trying to steal his house,* and finally, "You're *not* my girlfriend you know."

"I am aware. In fact, to give you credit, you did tell me long ago you didn't think you could really love anybody."

Then, he actually did ask me *what I'd do if he just changed the locks.*

"I'd get a restraining order on you" came out of me so fast that he *had* to know I'd thoroughly reviewed all of my options, and he must have known… *I was well aware he's been doing the same.*

He volleyed back off that one by asking when *I would sign off on the house.*

I said I'd do it *when I was ready to make a move.*

He said something like, *if I was just afraid he'd evict me, he would never do that… if I paid the utilities, etc.*

"Wish I could trust you, but you told me that *your crew* would drive the work truck …if I signed off on that, and look who lied."

He got to jumping up and down in front of me, repeating, "*FUCK YOU, FUCK YOU, FUCK YOU*" until saliva came rolling out the corner of his mouth.

Really, I had to laugh. I shouted a few more key points above his screaming. *Maybe he should actually try working through his past issues because I'm pretty convinced that is the issue here.* I went on, but who knows how much of it landed? So, I went back to the basement to work on other things.

An hour or so later, he came around admitting that taking care of that long overdue child support bill has got to be his top priority.

"Thank you, Jesus," I say. "That's the reason God has let you have such a booming business you know… so you can get this stuff taken care of."

"I know it."

We'll see where this goes. If having the guts to stand your ground counts for anything, I probably lost or gained quite a bit of ground right here, depending on how he sees it.

"When we see that our moods, views, and insights are transitory, we acquire a sense of movement, a current of change in our lives. This current, or river, is a flow of grace moving us to our right livelihood, companions, and destiny." I know that, at least, I wasn't afraid of him anymore, and that's worth a lot.

CHAPTER SIX

*"And still after all this time, the Sun has never said to the Earth,
'You owe me.' Look what happens with love like
that. It lights up the sky." —Rumi*

Last Sunday, he left the house to go see his Dad... *again*, without me. Then, he calls me from the Home Depot along the way. "What do you think about us putting up Christmas lights this year?"

"Awesome."

When he got home, he not only brought a movie, he asked me if I *wanted to go see his Dad later.*

"Of course."

It was a little weird when I first got in his truck. He led off with some comment suggesting I was in a seat of honor and to not get used to it. I spit something back, but we cut the shit pretty quick.

I love his Dad, and his Dad loves me. So, I was very pleased to spend some time there. In fact, it happened to be a terrific female entertainer there that night. I really enjoyed it. My good mood stayed well into the next day ... enough to drive home a point for me ...*that creativity needs to be fed.*

Thanksgiving rolls around. This is the last day weather-wise probably where we can get the outside work we need to do done... for a better insurance coverage. Joe gets on it early, and we did very well together. But then he asked me what time I was going out to my brothers. I said, "Aren't you coming with me?"

"No, I'm not."

I didn't say a word. Things have been wrong with us for so long, I'd already mentally prepared myself for this. It isn't hard to discern several ulterior motives. But regardless of which *exact* reasoning was behind it, the *no reaction* seemed the best all around. Anything I say can be turned on me, so *not* worth the risk.

Also, he normally really likes my older brother, but he had put a call into him a few weeks back and didn't get a return call. Joe is still at such a fragile point in his recovery; even completely innocent slights are magnified beyond belief. I just now found out my brother has significant short-term memory loss, so I'm guessing that's probably what happened, by the way.

Plus, I have been mentally wrestling a little bit about possibly making an amends to Joe …about the remark I made last week that my daughter can't stand him. Basically, she thought the world of him until she talked to him at the VFW one day last year when he was drinking. She never did tell me exactly what he said, but evidently, it was along the lines of how *I will never be his girlfriend,* and God only knows what the *Why* was he delivered to her. *She does not know how unimportant the why is though.* She has no idea that in his current state, no one can ever really earn his trust, *because it is he who feels so unworthy.*

So, for whatever reason, he didn't come with to the Thanksgiving Dinner. I'm pretty sure that he ultimately justified it with *"I'm not his girlfriend."*

This, by the way, is a statement he juxtapositions with *"I do love you, you're my best friend."* I am *his* best friend when he *needs* something. Not, however, when there's something fun to do. So yes, this is sick.

And since it is so sick, I do have to get out. All I can say at this point is that if it *does* work out, it will have to be all God because I don't think I even want to try at all anymore. This is apparently his sentiment as well because the bottom line of his behavior reads on a pretty plain and regular basis lately… *I want you to leave.*

One reason for coupling up in the first place may have been my *assumed* stability. Now maybe he needs to show the world he can do it on his own, which includes not going to meetings anymore either.

This is sounding so harsh. I've been thinking a lot about the dual personality piece of this disease too. The people with the best success continually work a tight program because it's the best deterrent to steer away from the stinking thinking part of it. Once we get ourselves over into the negative ruts, it isn't easy to switch back up into the positives. Our ruts are deep.

I feel like I really am dealing with dry drunk syndrome here, both *mine* and *his*. Al-Anon literature says to detach emotionally. I went to thanksgiving supper without him. I called my daughter on the way and cried a little bit to her. She was sweet. Also, I brought the dog, so I had reason to leave early. I had good conversations, I had a great meal, and I came home.

On the way home, it was the first snow of the year. I was sad remembering a Sunday morning drive to a church service with him a few years back. It was a lot like this. We both really got into it. I waxed nostalgic. I missed him.

A few fights back, when I was so sick of his same old twisted bullshit, I screamed something that came out lame— like *You're just so frickin' old*— at him several times. I'm older that he is by a few years, so that's pretty funny.

Anyway, after that, he suddenly started wearing hats. One, in particular, *does not do anything for him*. I realize there's no way to tell him that. Just as there is no way to tell him it's not his baldness that I meant... that was old looking to me... it's his *bullshit*.

He has told me many times that he tried and tried to earn his ex-wife's love and that he just was not able to do it. *This* he attributed to his baldness. I'm guessing this probably had very little to do with it. His sexually dysfunctional *attitude* makes me believe that they both played a million games with each other... so their egos would survive the pain and hurt.

His baldness is such a part of which he is; I wouldn't change it for the world. So, since he was being such a shit today and I needed to feel better, I took the hat that I really don't like and threw it in the garbage. It made me feel so much better, and I did not overeat.

But who knows? It might be my thing too. I did tell him that I'm leaving in a couple years when my credit straightens out, just to show him how detached I am . . . a fight or so ago. Maybe he figures, *why bother with her relatives?*

In all reality, when they called and invited us, I said yes without asking him. I just told him we were invited, period. And because we have such a hard time with basic discussion these days, I didn't even approach learning the details for his dad's nursing home thanksgiving program. I told my family that he had to go to his Dad's, implying it was a semi-crisis.

Joe has actually stated to me many times that he knows no one will stay with him indefinitely. So, I wonder what makes him able to realize *step one,* so to speak, that *he has a problem yet not* have the motivation to work on solution.

I know God can do anything. Through him, nothing is impossible, and I really do care so much about Joe. He does try to understand how and where he's misusing his potential. I do know that he is a Christian, and there is a chance that his true calling will be to lead the way for those life-long addicts to *finally* find serenity and a recovery that works. I'm not anywhere near working through my shortcomings, but the less and less addiction in my life, the more I have been able to follow my dreams. The steps you know *underpin* what can become a magnificently beautiful staircase.

I've also spent time thinking over the history of romance. It is only recently that people married for love. I started thinking about the great torch burning songs…all the way from Dionne Warwick's *"Why do you have to be a Heart breaker"* to now Pink's *"You gotta get up and try, try, try."* This is an area of pain for all of society evidently. My favorite philosopher to quote about relationship insights, *Rumi,* was from the thirteenth century. Suffice it also say the topic's been around a while.

I took a few notes last week while I was watching the Joyce Meyers program about *pressing and making right choices even while we are hurting.* Once I decide to operate in God's economy, I will get rewarded. Basically, get over your past and your self-pity, *or* be miserable. Refuse to give up, and you will receive double for your trouble.

…when I *Good Morning* him in a pleasant tone the next day, I get:

"So, how'd your Thanksgiving go?"

"Very, very nice, and by the way, I realize that your never did actually say you would go, I just assumed you would because you told me several times you wanted to do something with them. You were missed, but I told them we probably wouldn't see much of you until your Dad dies."

I updated him with the news items from their world. When I was telling him about their new cabin needing insulation, he said he'd *give him a call be-*

cause he's got just the guy to do it for him. From there, the rest of the day was polite and respectful. Interesting stuff, I tell you, this sweeping my side of the street approach.

So now his boss' Christmas party/annual business meeting weekend is upon us. He had originally said he was going out there on Friday night to spend a little time visiting with his daughter nearby, in the same trip. Actually, it was an invitation sent to me, as well as the bookkeeper, but *obviously*, he didn't want me to go.

Friday night as I head out to do my thing, he does ask what I'm up to. He's still there when I get back after 10pm. Saturday morning, he's up early doing his laundry. I ask if he plans on taking the dog to see if I can glean any details. "No."

I get dressed and decide I should go buy groceries, so I can have a roast in the oven while I'm at an art car parade later. I am struggling to hide my emotions.

I can't focus very well.

But I want to look as well as I can for his parting view. I decide to grab my all-time favorite gloves to wear. These white fur beauties are in p*erfect vintage shape.* I had got them out the night before to make sure I'd have them for this day's parade.

My clothes have been too tight lately to get a lot of satisfaction from my outfits, but these gloves were a *quantum-leap find...* just this last summer. They are capable of singlehandedly changing my mood. *Imagine the thrill... when I have them on both hands!*

"Load up," I say to the dog. We drive past Joe, who was going out to his truck. I never look up. I've got things to do. I turn the radio up, find my best sunglasses, check my lipstick, and get going.

Well, now, it turns out to be a nice day. I feel empowered in the grocery store. My body feels strong. I only buy what's good for me. Life is good.

When I get back out to my car, I find *the dog has chewed my beautiful vintage gloves into a million pieces.* I feel absolutely insane. I put the groceries in the trunk. I gather the hopeless mess into a plastic bag and take it to a garbage can.

I am not even *able* to choke back my full-scale sobbing in the parking lot. I get in the car and grab the long-handled windshield scrapper. I turn around *and beat the hell out of our dog* in the backseat. He yelps hard and loud on the first few rounds then just gives up to the hopeless of it. He can't escape, so he tries to just curl into an invisible, quiet ball. The look of *that* infuriates me further. I know what I am doing is going way too far, but I turn around and throw another round of good hard hits…several more times…before we get home.

I am aware that a large part of this level of anger is my frustration with Joe, but I am also aware that I've had a temper like this whole life. I'm in a good mood for the vast amount of time, but when I'm mad, I'm crazy. Chances are that this ties directly into with *my* addiction issues… the levels of neurotransmitters and all that. Plus, I believe the average person would be so *repulsed* by this behavior in me that they would find it hard to forgive me and that this is *possibly* another area only addicts can understand.

Please … I do ask the dog and the world to forgive me. Yet, I am aware that I am also responsible to take steps to ensure that things like this never happen again. Sure, I shouldn't have left them in the car in the first place. *Never mind that to have a dog protect me, I have to constantly be vigilante of a lot of things I suddenly have to protect from it.*

The world, I am sure, will cast its vote that *finally ending the Joe situation will provide the best solution all around.* I spent time reviewing that option again in my head. Really, I have a Chapter 13 Judgment on me for a couple more years, and I'm still paying back a hefty school loan. I cannot live anywhere else cheaper. But I do also have a survival instinct, and God will direct this for me *if I listen.*

The house is currently in my name, and I've put heart and soul into it. But I figure a restraining order on him would dangle me as *a murder candidate* if it meant *he* was forced to move out. I am for real about this.

One of his favorite shows is some murder mystery program *about this kind of thing.* I'm not a fan, so I don't know the exact name of the program. Plus, *he just bought his daughter a pistol.* It does occur to me that this entire story looks a lot like the scripts leading up to the murders on this show. I spend time almost frozen in this ominousness. It is, in fact, a very bleak moment of emotional terror.

Thus, I did give myself a very stern talking too. I reminded myself that I recently asked him *if I should be worried that he watches such things on TV.* He very calmly came back with, "You really are shallow about *that show* because if you pay attention, it's always about how they *don't get* away with it."

Good to know. Also, kudos to him are in order since he didn't go *completely* black and white with his thinking towards me here. There have been times when he's said I was way too shallow, *period.* Nice that he has addressed it in a more behavior specific way. The *it's just my attitude towards this television show* tells me that he has actually been hearing me about some of the all or nothing stuff I've been laying on him, right?

I also would like to point out that he has now been abstinent for over a year and has had a lot of excellent things happen to him. He's hooked up with quality work, and his business is really making money. I, on the other hand, have not had anything close to 1 year of abstinence with my food plan program for several years now. So, heads up to me, I guess.

And as another aside here, the gal I invited to ride along with me in the art parade the day he went to that Christmas Party had asked me to provide the impetus for her to make an art car. I decided to give my very best selection of canvases to her to mount on to the older motorhome; thus, a true art-car. I had gleaned them off of Craig's list. The son of a University art teacher had so many of his Mom's paintings; he was giving them away to be painted over. I never had the heart to do that, so I kept them waiting for something as awesome as *this* plan to use them for.

I noticed this gal wasn't very far on this project when I picked her up. We were in the middle of the parade when she non-nonchalantly mentions to me that got $95.00's a piece for those canvases. I am *mortified,* but I kept cool and processed. I said nothing, but I felt like this was *dirty low life bullshit.*

Later in the afternoon, Joe did call me to say he really got a nice bonus and to double check about some of business. I told him what I was miffed about, and he does fall right in with the empathy skills I want and need. Plus, I think it does him good to know *he's not the only person I see as an occasional low life-form.*

Sunday, he leads off with a conversation to me about how he's pushing to get a company office in this neighborhood. I am not sure if this is idle chit chat or if it's meant to be an area where my thoughts are valued. Also … is it to be something I will become a part of?

Then, he surprised me with *"so … what do you want for Christmas this year?"*

I paused and lifted my shoulders enough to indicate *no real idea.* But I came back with *"Tell your boss to find us a house that's not on a hill, with a big enough front room for an office."* After I put that idea out here, I went about my projects, hoping he realizes this means I still want to live with him in case he was wondering.

Some schools of thought see making each other *better people* as the point of love. I don't know if all that's true. But I have to say that he has such good listening skills, a true appreciation for my creativity, and he does usually leave me alone to do it. I see *these* are all very important to me. Dear, God, please, I pray that we can help rebuild each other into better new selves.

Out of the blue, then later in the day while he was out running errands, he calls to tell me *he has a kind of wild idea.*

"Uh, oh."

"I know it," he giggles.

"What?"

"What about trying to move stuff around to put a Christmas tree?"

"Cool." I hope I say with enough *cover in my voice* to process this in its entirety.

I told him awhile back that I had 10 days off over Christmas. My whole extended family is going to the farm this year because my sister and her family are coming from Texas. I want to take the camper. He said he had *other plans.*

"So," I say, "is your daughter coming or something?"

"Nooo… nobody's coming." But then, big muffled noise… and we get cut-off.

Later, I call back and ask if he is coming to the farm with me, and he very nicely says, "Don't count on it."

When he gets home, we return to the possibility of re-arranging for a tree. One thing leads to another, and he tells me that we need to have a really serious talk soon. He's in a good mood and wants to stay that way, so he says we'll do it a different night. I say, "No, what? Let's get it out."

He hasn't been able to sleep at night, he tells me, since I let him know I won't just sign the house over to his daughter until I was ready. So, right back into the whole when and how argument. *This* stressor, he tells me, *is why he doesn't go places with me…*on and on *this* goes.

I tell him that I can't really even sign a paper saying *if something should happen to me, then it goes to his daughter* because then he would be tempted to kill me. He tells me how crazy I am. I tell him I have everything documented. I grabbed an earlier of *this* document, laid it on him, and went to bed.

*****

Well, Christmas came and went now. I had a really good time up at the farm for several days. I get the impression that his time back here wasn't *that* fabulous. He did buy me some really nice presents, and I see he put some thought into it too. So, it's touch and go, day by day, play it by ear. Several comfortable days went by. We talked about what needed to happen to finish the remodel on this house. He tells me everything has to be out to do it.

The next day, he says he's more than willing to give me down payment money to get a contract for deed house somewhere while they're cheap. I tell him that *wow, as soon as I can land somewhere like that safely, I will sign the house over to his daughter. He can even stay there as long he needs to until he gets the re-model done here.*

Then, one day he calls me at work to see if I can do a special billing that night for him. Next, he casually mentions that he's going to his older brother's to buy a really nice snowmobile that upcoming weekend. Well, he went and got it, and he dropped by his daughter's for a visit as well. I was cordial about the whole thing. *"Yes, it's nicely. Really nice."* He didn't even have anywhere to put it, so he had to rent a garage for it.

Plus, it's *not* really making me believe that he's trying to pay off the child support bill, but again, it's not my place to say anything about that. He does work really hard, and so who knows? Maybe he does deserve it. But I suspect the true motivator for him is an almost insatiable need *to look like he's doing great financially.*

Soon after he came back from that weekend, he mentions to me that his daughter's coming up in about 10 days or so to do the paperwork on the house. This *stops me in my tracks.* While I did tell him that I'd sign off on it, I also said *"as soon as I could get re-situated."*

What I had told him was that I'd go back to school online and finish my Master's Degree to get extra school loan cash built up. This I would save to use in case I could come across a Contract for Deed. A conversation that clearly indicated at least a period of another six months before I could make any kind of move.

So yes, this *six months turning ten days* was a stressor for me. I think the true issue behind this was that he just *always has to have some big wonderful thing to offer up to whoever he's trying to impress at the time.* Currently, it is his daughter. Plus, I'm fairly certain that she has no immediate plans to move to this area, so it's not like I'm being thrown out.

But… I have heard *get the fuck out of my house* so many times now that I cannot trust him when he tells me that I am welcome to stay even after signing it over if I pay the utilities. Default behavior is default behavior. Once I sign it over, the very next temper tantrum could easily put me on the street. I tell him I am not signing it over in the next 10 days.

He tries to work his way into, *but I just sat here last week and told him I'd do it.* I argue back with the point about what *my time frame was on that statement.* I can see that now it's more of an embarrassment issue for him since he'd made it such a big deal.

That week was a little tense. Then one night, he brought home a new supply of nice Tupperware. He just left them setting on the counter. I thanked him for such a nice offering. I then proceeded to put them away.

Here's where the story gets dicey, so let me give a little background. As I have stated, this is a small house with crowded quarters. I had a nice sturdy old-fashioned ice cream chair that I kept in a corner of the kitchen because it worked perfectly for many things, including using it as stepstool to reach the upper cupboards. Granted, it blocked a few rarely used spots, but it was easy to move if you needed to. It also provided a surface area for things like recharging electronics in a house where a lot of plug-ins don't work. My cost/benefits analysis was that *it was worth it to keep it there and big deal… this is not a showplace by any means.*

When he was on one of his high horses a few months back, he determined that this chair was in the way and that it had to go somewhere else. To minimize that fury, I moved it somewhere else. A few days after that, he brought home this little narrow table thing and said we can put it in that spot. Okay.

Now on this night, I can see that putting away the Tupperware is going to be a time-consuming ordeal because the entire top shelf will have to be rearranged first. Not only that, the way the house is set up, it's a straight view from his command centrally placed recliner to the kitchen. It is always a little unpleasant to work in there when you can feel his critical eye just waiting for any sign of clumsy, etc., and with hands full of degenerative arthritis, it happens.

But I shall persevere. I know that standing on this narrow little table is not a good idea, but I feel like I can't make a production out of it either because it may have been a peace offering for nixing my preferred chair there. I attempt to sort through this top shelf, all the while feeling like this make-shift step stool is teetering. I am silently praying that I don't crash it to pieces.

Then, suddenly, it *does go over,* and it breaks the dog dish into a million pieces. As I am cleaning up this big mess, he tells me that I shouldn't be using that *as a step-stool.* I blow back at him hard. "The problem is that chair I had there *was* there for a reason, and it's coming right back here!"

He comes back harder. "You fat cunt," he says to me, and then I don't know what else. This is the first time I have ever heard either of those words directed at me from him. I know somewhere in there I managed to say to him, "What's the deal anyway with that being possibly the only problem you *don't* suffer from, and yet it's the first thing you point out as wrong in others? What's that about?" I know it made him think a little, but we were totally into the hot heads stage… so, off we go.

I see that this is really about it being only a week or so till his daughter comes, and his noble offering to her is not yet *secured.* It gets really bad. I remember even getting in his face *again*, with both middle fingers up stiff as can be, while I shout, "Cunt! Cunt!" right back at him. Now, if the truth be told, I did not take great offense at the word cunt. I think that by throwing that word back at him, I am covering the fact that the word *fat* hurts much worse.

Really, since I put on these extra pounds, he would find little ways to try to hint to me about it. But somehow, he always stopped short of actually calling me out on it. However, as I hang around the rooms of overeaters anonymous, I do hear women tell about times where the significant other has set them down and told them the extra weight is a turn–off. I probably could give him credit for trying to be as decent as he possibly can about it for years now and that he's made it this far, really. But I don't … because I think I need to *not show him that it hurts.* Neither of us is well enough emotionally to be trusted with big ammunition of any sort.

Then, he goes off in his room… *door shut.* Through the door, I kind of tried to apologize for my part of the temper tantrum. I go into a spiel about the cramped quarters here, etc. I calmly re-suggest to him that maybe he should try to see if one of the millionaires he works for has some kind of a place I could rent with the option to buy etc. Then, I just go to bed, get up the next day, and go to work.

Saturday morning, when I came up from the basement, Joe had his back to me and was slowly mixing sugar into his coffee. He was in no hurry to move, so I couldn't get to either. Then, as I stood in the stairwell waiting for him, I could tell right through his pajamas bottoms that the muscles in his butt were set in a very firm resolution about something.

This may seem like a strange observation, but this man has the graceful kind of body you normally see in paintings of the back sides of bullfighters. The form of their derriere has a language of its own.

"I rented a house yesterday," he says to me, still not turning around.

"Oh."

Thankfully, I had already planned to head to the gym. I had an escape route available to go and start processing *this big news.* He tells me a few details but landed on "don't get me wrong, I'm not giving you *this* house."

"I have no doubt of that."

He said he'd rent it to me for $750, and I offered back $500 a month *and I get signed off of his truck and his bank account. I want it clean.* He accepted. Foremost on my thoughts to process list here is that God is at the helm. This news is undoubtedly a very good thing.

Is this then the end of a relationship that I have invested a lot in? I'm hoping the shock will cushion me till I can really feel it and grieve. Yet, at the same time, I find myself rearranging the house *in my head* with a great deal of new satisfactory comfort for me.

A lot transpired as he proceeded to get moving by the time his daughter did come that next weekend. Plus, somewhere in there, the story changed. He started telling people that *he bought this other house.* Has he forgotten that he originally told me he was renting it? He never even mentions insurance coverage, etc. for it. Plus, I had to sign on the one we are at, so he wouldn't have it taken away for the child support bill. *Why would owning a new house be any different?*

I'm thinking he did go try to see if there was something for me to rent, and when he saw that one, he wanted it for himself. It has the stainless steel and granite kitchen, the earth toned tiled bathroom, etc. It is the style of renovation his company is cranking out these days almost by rote. So yes, it is a nicely re-done house. We were about to kill each other, something had to give. He's making good money; let him go do whatever.

The weekend came. That Saturday was surreal. As we packed up his stuff, everyone was very polite. He'd say to his daughter things like *and every week as we'd go to the grocery store, we'd stop and browse the thrift shop for these little collectables.* We were both very generous to each other in the give and take process involved in splitting up.

He even invited me to come along with him and his daughter to go get his new stuff and then come over to the new house hang around for the putting it together party, but I left after 5 minutes.

I am aware of the impulse control issues involved with the disease of alcoholism, and I'm pretty sure this whole thing went down as just that. I don't really think his moving out is all about me as much as needing to have a place that wasn't in so much need of remodeling completion. And he just has to try to impress people. So…*whatever* …I can't wait to turn his room into my new office.

His daughter likes me a lot. She rode with me in my car to the furniture store that day. It could have been kind of awkward since he's certainly been dissing me to his family lately. I'm sure he has twisted the story quite a bit. *Oh well… is my vindicator.*

The rent I pay to stay here is to be paid to his daughter. He's making her a partner in his business. I am also aware that he is thinking that when I sign a renter's agreement, it will provide the leg to stand on which he's looking for, that this will show legal ownership of the house… as theirs. I still do not trust him enough yet to have signed a quick claim on this house.

When I'm feeling magnanimous enough to separate the person from the disease, I get into a mental exercise in my head where I try to discern what constitutes adaptive behavior and what defines maladaptive behaviors. I get this whole picture of his early horrific poverty as the spring board he operates from. Like maybe *an item of worth* is gifted and then re-gifted as many times as necessary to *survive.* And I do see this as being much different than the run of the mill *give to get* type of thought process.

"I know the house is yours, and I'll take good care of it," was my lead in statement to his daughter in the car that day. I went on to explain that I just needed *leverage* to try to get him to clean up some of the other areas he has to deal with. Also, I tell her that I think he just needs to do his thing by himself right now.

She is nodding accordingly, so I continue. I tell her he's the best person I've ever met and that he treats people like gold. I give her *playbacks* of conversations he has with tenants in the properties he manages, etc. *Never a finer person ever made, but then his dual personality kicks in, and look-out.* I catch myself tearing up, and I see she is too. "I'm not telling you anything you don't know." And I leave it there.

So, he moved out. I shifted things around here very comfortably. I painted the kitchen floor to match a color in the funky floral walls, and I love it. The floor in the bathroom had gobs of old tile broken off but still glued solid to the floorboards, so what to do here? Aha…*wow…* it turned out a leopard skin fur floor is just the ticket. Suffice it to say…I love my new digs.

CHAPTER SEVEN

"Gamble everything for love, if you are a true human being. If not, leave this gathering. Half-heartedness doesn't reach into majesty."—Rumi

I am still taking care of business for him though. Surprise and surprise. And he has now made comments indicating he may have re-evaluated his views on some things about us and my book, both. He pointed out how he is listening to music so much more now, and put in a Celine Dion CD in to prove it. Plus, as he reached something for me, I hear a side comment about how his *long arms* are good for something. Both incidences seemed to be referring to information he had gleaned from reading what he did… of the rough draft of this.

He has sent a crew over to shovel snow here for me many times now. He has put new doors on this house, front and back. He called just to tell me I'd be so proud of him; he finally got a current ID. He is starting to make lists when he runs out of things…*just like I do.*

Then one day, I saw a pretty decent duplex in the paper listed as Contract for Deed. I start to think that maybe I should be making payments instead of paying rent. The rental agreement I signed with his daughter here states that I can leave sooner if I choose too. Joe added that in to be nice to me, by the way.

When I talked about looking at this other house, Joe offered to get me the cash for the up-front money. He accompanied me on the inspections and helped with the paperwork details. He has invited me to lunch a few times.

Also of note, he has touched me in a very loving way, just on my shoulder, when the realtor was being friendly with me. He makes sure the guy knows we've lived together. However, I am aware that he really, really has a thing for Bergen, the activities director at the nursing home his Dad moved into several months back. Joe bragged to me how she had his dad living it up and drinking on Friday nights now. Then, Joe received a hanging lamp she made when he moved into his own place. He made a point to show it to me. Not really to rub it in my face either… *more just to show me something that was awesome.* It is absolutely a dainty, graceful, delicate, and beautiful work of art.

The boundary issue thing crosses my mind here. What if his Dad receives favoritism at the nursing home due to his son's magnetic powers, etc.? Really though, if I had a job like that, I would absolutely *treasure* a volunteer that makes things as lively as *he* can. Joe thoroughly enjoys making *everyone* feel special. It is his greatest gift.

Anyway, Joe messed up and accidentally sent an email *meant for her…* to me. I have enough clues to indicate that the feelings and emotions rumbling around here are quite an obsession.

Some of this I based on my own prior experience of a torturous affairs with a married man. And some of it is based on the context of what I know about Joe's life through observations, key points in his stories, and points of view. *We* haven't had sex for three years or so now, and I seriously doubt that he's had too much on the side either in that time.

He's made no real effort to pay-off his outstanding child support bill, so *legally* hooking in with *anyone* would kill their credit too. What's a man in his situation to do? Never mind that he has pissed away more than enough to pay that bill in the last six months.

I have really tried to understand this. Maybe because he grew up with such an extreme level of poverty, the idea of actually getting to the top of the bill pile *legitimately* seems completely unrealistic, so he just tries to fit his fun in when he can… and the hell with the rest of it.

Maybe he has decided the whole dog and pony show *of needing to manipulate others* into covering his bases for him is actually easier to do, or maybe that's all he currently knows *how* to do. He is an incredibly hard worker, but he is also drawn to get rich quick schemes. Plus, he gets in real trouble, *usually* when things are going good for him. Then, he gets into playing the big-shot, and he is *just compelled to be overly generous, and he cannot stop himself.* Thus, more humility and the cycle will continue to perpetuate.

As long as I'm on bones of contention, I'd like to go on record that the treatment programs he's attended *do nothing to address issues like that either.* God only knows how much baggage he's really still carrying around from way back when.

He can be so kind and fun and generous that I wish him some peace. I am fairly certain he has very little of that right now because his *using behavior* always just comes down to sounding like the *little boy whistling in the dark.* Dear God, please help him.

*****

Last Monday morning, his whole right side was numb when he got up. *He thought he'd had a stroke.* I see by the bank statement he'd had quite a wild weekend. He was so scared; he actually *did* go in for tests. Alas, it was *not* a stroke, but most likely a pinched nerve, and it's not so good.

His *at least emotional* love affair has such a flavor of obsession on it that I doubt too much good will come of it. And I'm really sad for him about it. I get the feeling his latest *staging* at the new place will blow up in his face here pretty soon. Two weekends in a row, he has lost his cell-phone, and we have spent hours the following Monday mornings getting something up and running again for him.

Anyway, the closer it came to closing on the duplex I had an offer on, the more I knew I really *couldn't* depend on Joe to help with the stuff that needed to get done there. Plus, I knew he didn't have the money to give me I needed for closing. Finally, I acted out quite the fit where I re-directed the blame to some other aspect just to get out of it.

I think Joe thought I wanted that house *more* than I really did. He felt bad about it I know. *My* real issue is that I am worried that sooner or later he will get evicted from his trendy new place. Then what? While I was *stewing about really not wanting him to come back here,* I am happy to report that the *still small voice* in me *whispered.* I feel like I am getting spiritual breakthroughs these days, where I can trust that the right thing will happen.

The Behavior Analyst in me has been watching and listening to how Joe goes about constructing meaning and determining what is important, for years now. I have tried to be sensitive to the changing meanings he feels as different emotions flow through him, and I have sought for the deep understanding of whatever he was experiencing, be it fear or rage or tenderness or confusion.

While I would very much like to report to you that all of this *attending* was done while moving about in it delicately and without making judgments, that is, of course, not true. Many times, my approach was very unorthodox to Al- Anon Principles and other principles in general. But now, lately, I'm much more in tune with myself just trying to work my own program. My favorite *definition of co-dependency,* by the way, is that *you just plain are not doing your own self- care.* Interesting, huh?

While on the other hand, I do feel I have a pretty good grasp of the central issues in his life, *as well as the spin he gives them*, I think I may have fallen short on how to respond to them. Yes, yes, yes. Many times I would detect the gaps and distortions in the stories and mentally note them, only *to just file them away* for a more appropriate time to challenge him about it.

It is also important to point out here that he is, by nature, so *generous*, that he has given away much more than the accumulated amount of old interest he owes on that child support bill. Seriously, he sends money even to his extended family to make ends meet. He hands it over right and left to his daughter in offerings and even to strangers in need. Sometimes, I wonder though if he unconsciously uses this to justify *why it's okay to do life his way.*

Maybe I should have tried to better relay *the hopelessness of self-pity* for one thing. At times, his need to talk about the unfair experiences in his life over and over again sort of became a way for him to also avoid taking the responsibility to rise above them. I was relatively good at weaving some of my perceptions into dialogue with him, but when I saw things *such as* the self-pity slanting itself through a story, I did *not* share my hunches with him or challenge him much about it, possibly out of intimidation or maybe even confusion about how to go about al-anon styled detachment. Then again, we are all just learning and doing the best we can.

Yet, I am also coming to realize that accurate perceptions are meaningless if they are not communicated. *Few* people *do* know how to put empathetic understanding into words. Thus, this then becomes another reason for the rendering of this book. I have found my voice. Maybe someday I'll give him a finished copy. I have changed the names, used a penname, and forewent identifying factors because I do respect his anonymity. I did my research, and I don't want to get sued.

He will know it is us. And even if his first reaction isn't wonderful, I don't care. At least I will have done my part to communicate these perceptions the best I could because I hope it helps. Carl Ransom states that the therapeutic relationship is only a special instance of interpersonal relationships in general and that the same lawfulness governs *all* such helping relationships. He goes on to state that his bottom line question which he asks himself when he encounters troubled and conflicted people is *how can I provide a relationship which this person may use for his own personal growth?*

I am not really trying to give a little psych class here, but I feel it is important to note that this world renowned therapist has come to the conclusion that "it is only by providing the genuine reality which is in me, that the other person can successfully seek for the reality in him… even when the attitudes do not seem conducive to a good relationship. We need to be real."

Joe moved out *several* months ago now, but he still needs me for bookwork and banking until his daughter gets things transferred over; *this week now*, he tells me, *it will happen for sure*. He calls almost daily, and I see him several times a week. I know that he has been struggling since he has fallen back into using. I know he is scared.

On Easter Sunday, when he called me at 3am because of some off- hand comment I'd made to him earlier in the day, he told me he'd been obsessing about it all day and then couldn't sleep. I tried to convince him that it was *nothing*, and that wasn't easy.

I find that I mostly feel very warm regard for him as a person of unconditional self-worth. He has value and potential no matter what the fluctuating aspect of his disease happens to be at the time, or his behavior, or his feelings. I do want him to experience the safety of being loved and prized as a person. So, I remind him of his greatness when it seems as though he is in some kind of frightening search for himself.

For example, no one in this world ever had more tender loving care than he just gave his step- mom earlier this year, *for months on end,* while on her death bed. It was beauty to behold. It was him just pouring out 100% pure love. *"If you have some respect for people as they are, you can be more effective in helping them to become better than they are."*-John W. Gardner

I cannot imagine having anyone greater than this around for old age after witnessing such a thing. Still, at this juncture, I am happy *not* to live with him. I am happy to sit here in peace and write without the television, going no smoking and constant jabbering on the phone.

By the way, honesty about things such as this, they say, will provide a climate conductive to promoting maturity all around. And supposedly, wanting to be mature is an innate tendency in us all. I tell him when I have other plans and can't help do something right then. We have at least been treating each other more respectfully now… most of the time.

Last night, he called to tell me that he would be over in the morning with the plumber because something was wrong with the drain in the basement. I knew he was pretty loaded because he was telling me how much he loved me in every other sentence. His final statement was that *in the morning, we'd go to Menards and get a new kitchen sink and cabinet besides!*

So, I got up and just kept busy all morning, knowing the plan may or may not transpire. Joe calls then, finally, at about 11am. I hear some *chick* in the background, and I realize that he has his phone speaker on the side, *just so I can hear him talking to her.* I try to ask about when *and if* the plumber is coming.

Then, Joe raunches out some line about how *I probably shouldn't be doing his help.* This is followed by his canned uproarious laughter. Then he says, "Are you laughing?"

I hear more drunken *who-ha* with the girly. She starts talking then. Something in a staggering voice about "she's the girl *with* him… who am I?" I hear Joe cut in, "Oh she don't like that you're here, I know that."

It was so obvious that he was purposely trying to make sure I knew that. I simply didn't care because what it really told me was how wasted he was. This

This is a man, *who in his right mind*, abhors crass. And yes, I can hear the little slutty making as much noise as possible, trying to get in the game too.

"I'm the girl he calls when he only *gets* one call."

Dead silence, so I add, "Are you laughing?"

It takes a moment, but he gives a weak "yeah." Then, he starts making some case about my being jealous, I *assume*…but I cut right through it hard core.

"How in God's name do you plan to get this stopped again? Do you have a plan? Are you going to go back to meetings, or what?" I out and out scream at him.

He comes back with soft, weak murmurings of, "Hey, I'll be alright, you know how much I love you, blah, blah, blah."

I just hang up. But you know what? Maybe I am getting more mature. I decided to send him an email.

"By now I hope you know… I do have at least a relative understanding of what it is like to not be able to stop…unless I crash and burn.

But I have been thinking about how, after the first edition of the Big Book, they re-wrote it so that not everyone has to crash and burn every time. It became enough for them to see the hopelessness of the pattern before all was lost and reach out for help.

Thus, I am asking you if you think there may be even a remote possibility that this time maybe, before all is lost, would you at least consider trying something like a day at a Hospital, tomorrow even…and then get a sponsor and a meeting plan and just really try to work the program that way? I also think just to do a 4Th and 5TH step would be such a tremendous burden lifted off of you. I have to say, I'd love to see you try.

Also, I am sending an attachment of an article from the Fix magazine that I think you should read about how much relief people are getting in their sobriety because they are finally using the correct psycho-tropic medications for their ailments. Very successful and very interesting."

I sent it, and from there, it is out of my hands.

Hang on, this response just in: Good Morning, I hope that YOU KNOW I AM WORKING A PROGRAM THAT WORKS FOR ME. I AM ALWAYS GOING TO BE THE ONE THAT NEVER QUITS BEING ME. SORRY YOU ARE SO DISAPPOINTED IN THE LIFE STYLE I LIVE, BUT TILL THE DAY I DIE, I AM GOING TO DO IT MY WAY. I AM ENJOYING LIFE TO THE MAX. DON'T WORRY ABOUT ME. I DO JUST FINE. NO CRASH AND BURN. JUST ENJOYING THE WEEKENDS.

People cultivate the *way of Life* that is spirituality *by seeking out those wanting to live the same way of life.* He is not ready to work a program of recovery. So be it. It seems like Joe hasn't fully surrendered and feels like he has to keep one foot in *both worlds.*

My friends, chances are great that Joe and I do not finally end up happily ever after with each other. Realistically, I am no more special to him than probably several of the other women that have been in this boat with him.

He overly shares with *a lot* of people because he doesn't have a handle on what intimacy really is. The bottom line here is that it is impossible to be in a relationship with someone who's abusing a substance because that then becomes their foremost love and comfort.

As addicts, all we really have is a daily reprieve contingent on the maintenance of our spiritual condition. By the grace of God, I also now have run across a letter written by Bill W. co-founder of AA stating in part: "I am a firm believer in both guidance and prayer. But I am fully aware and humble enough; I hope to see there may be nothing infallible about my guidance. *"The minute I figure I have got a perfectly clear pipeline to God, I have become egotistical enough to get into real trouble."*

So yes, I really did think that God was leading me to believe that maybe we should be together, etc. But hardship does produce greater endurance, and even though I may be disappointed over certain things, I know God will not disappointment me in the end. As long as I don't stop praying for God's will for me, I know God will do amazing things with my life.

I have made the effort to really dig into the root of my spiritual condition as it plays out for me to live in recovery. I want to live in a way that model's recovery as attractively as possible. And you know what they say will happen if we are painstaking about this?

We are going to know a new freedom and a new happiness. We will not regret the past nor wish to shut the door on it. We will comprehend the word serenity, and we will know peace.

No matter how far down the scale we have gone, we will see how our experience can benefit others. That feeling of uselessness and self-pity will disappear.

We will lose interest in selfish things and gain interest in our fellows. Self-seeking will slip away. Our whole attitude and outlook on life will change. Fear of people and economic insecurity will leave us. We will intuitively know how to handle situations that used to baffle us. We will suddenly realize that God is doing for us what we could not do for ourselves.

I've been working a *tight* overeaters' anonymous program again for a while. This led to an assignment to also work an al-anon sponsor. Ultimately, she felt it best I go with my instincts and put the cards on the table for Joe's dad, Frank, to review as well.

Finally, when Joe had overdrawn the check book the day after he'd been paid, I just plain heard too many *sniffing* sounds out of him during a phone call. Whatever he spent the money on seems to have gone up his nose. So, armed with sponsor pushing/ screaming at me, I did write out a letter to his Dad and then drive myself out to the nursing home to read it to him.

It took his Dad a minute to register that it was me, but then he was so happy to see me. I tell him I really need to talk some things through, but that I had to write it out so that I could focus. I barely got started on this when the door to his room flies open and in bounds Joe, whistling and happy *until he sees me.* Then, he stops cold. What are *you* doing here?" he asks, eyebrows all furrowed.

"I'm just trying to work through some stuff. You can stay and listen if you want, if fact, I think you should."

"Not right now. Dad's got a care conference to go to."

"Fine. I'll come back later," I say as I start for the door.

"Don't make it too long," Frank calls after me.

Once I get out in the hallway, I am dazed enough to head in the wrong direction. By the time I turn around, Joe has caught up with me. He tries to get some kind of explanation. All I can come up with is vague stuff about trying to work through my codependents issues. I am hoping and praying my heart won't jump out of my chest.

I go home. But I realize that I will have to get right back there that night and actually accomplish this mission *now*, or forever hold my peace. So, I go back that night, and we have a very nice long heart to heart. I read parts of the letter but then just tell him what's in it.

Dear Frank,

Good morning. I have missed you a great deal. I am happy when I do hear that you are doing quite well. I am sad that the situation seems to prevent me from actually visiting with you more. However, I cannot express enough how wonderful it is that you are still with us here on earth. I am happy to report that I am still very grateful to be here in your old house. It is homey and comfortable. Everything I really need is here…even the central air! I still thoroughly enjoy the yard. I cannot even tell you nice it is.

Anyway, I remember more than one occasion where you had taken me aside and asked me to look out for Joe as best I can. I think you know this was not really even something you need to ask of me because of course, it is what I wanted to do anyway. There are horrible symptoms that go hand in hand with the progression of the disease of alcoholism, like whether or not he can really be trusted to follow through on all of his good intentions, but he is still a genuinely loving person at the core. And I think we all know that.

I have struggled deeply over my role in his life and even what approach to take. For a long time, I was convinced that I needed to continue to try to just love him

94

into a healthier place around his intimacy issues, etc. Plus, I spent a long time being *hung-up* on that whole AA concept about not taking someone else's *inventory*. In essence, I really felt it was *always* the right thing to do, to just mind my own business and not broadcast his, etc.

I also want to point out that I have studied addiction. It is real, and it is not his fault that he has it. Chances are he was even born with it. It is a vicious, cruel, and debilitating disease. He has struggled mightily with it because he does suffer from it. I personally believe that all we get really is a daily reprieve, and to get that, you need to be as *vigilant* about this as you would if it were some other ailment that required daily medicines.

I remember going along on a counselor's appointment after his first run in treatment. They told Joe that his chances weren't that good. He has been plagued with this throughout much of his life. Yet he does have so much real potential, mostly because, no matter what, he truly does believe in God.

The most important thing I need to learn *now is when it is time to do something and when it is time to just let things happen.* Suffice it to say that I am writing this letter to you because I am feeling divinely led to do it.

When I signed on his vehicle for him, he was sober and making every attempt to try to make an honest and respectable living. But, as you know, Joe is a force to reckon' with when he's on defense. So now, I'm struggling with having the heart to *take him down*, so to speak, by turning him in. I am trying to learn Al-Anon as fast as I can to figure where and how I needed to detach, etc.

Also, at this point, Joe has told me that I am no longer welcome around his family! Who knows exactly who he told what to and why? I have wanted to talk all of this through with you for a long time. Now, finally, as I am almost hit over the head degree of seriousness behind all of this… I do see you as a very viable option to turn to.

I thank God for giving me the courage to do it and to try inform you about these things in the manner that they are intended… *for the good that could come of just plain truthfulness.*

By Easter, I knew beyond a shadow of a doubt that he was abusing substances again… although I've suspected it for a long time. I have tried to think through where all of this is headed, knowing how progressive Joe's illness is and what the possible outcomes probably are… as well as what my responsibilities are here. Obviously, I do not want the guilt should he get in an accident while impaired. Yet, how exactly I go about stopping it… is the real question.

I have researched it enough to know that *I could say that he stole the vehicle from me*…to absolve myself…but it still leaves him in jail…which is where he'd probably be if I just plain reported him for driving without a license.

But … I do not see his being in jail… as that great of an answer either. *I love that he visits you all the time… I do not want to see that have to stop! You are the one that would be hurt the most by that.*

So… letting you in on all the facts seems to be the answer. It is your perspective that I'm looking for …*as really you have the most to lose should he go to jail.* I've also learned interventions are very expensive and rarely work on people that have already been in treatment. I'm not sure if he can even get into a long-term treatment facility on just GA either.

Much as I would love to see his business just thrive, I have the sinking feeling that it is on a downhill slide. Joe seems to be much more surrounded now by users than people in recovery. I suspect it is just a matter of time before he could even be evicted. I am aware that he may never forgive me for cluing you in on all of this. I'm okay with that too… because I now, at least, feel like I did at least make an effort.

This is what I can come up with…to try to keep my deal with you…to do my best by Joe. Please let me know what you think I should do.

Love always,

Jolene

Therein lays the contents of our discussion. It was a tear jerker, I'll tell you that. He crouched in close with his wheelchair to get right up to my face and put his arm around me. "Honey, you have to go to the police station and turn him in. Change the locks and get a gun. He's never going to change. Don't worry about me. I'll be fine."

Promising *I'd at least check some of that out,* we said hurried goodbyes. I was scared that at any moment, I'd get caught out there again. I knew I was probably going to get banned from coming out there now too. That is sad. I do love that old goat. I've cried with him many times.

The police station turned out to be less than helpful. *We're not going to put an APB out on him. You'd have to call us when you know he parked at an establishment and just wait to see if someone is available to cruise over there and wait around until he comes out, etc.* Okay, well… good to know. I guess.

Joe, of course, *tried* to figure out what all was going down. I was able to at least bluff *some fear* into him…although for a man that can almost *emote cells* that seethe when he's mad… the fact that he didn't come completely unglued here also suggests expensive drugs in his system… which also tells me that *maybe finding the right medication would be an excellent area to pursue in the treatment of alcoholism all around.*

He denied overdrawing the checking account, but whatever. I made it clear that by Friday, I'd have the account closed, and I did just that. *"You've put me in a position where I have to cripple you… before you cripple us both."*

Evidently, he got the *lecture of a lifetime* from dad then the following weekend. Joe called me crying as he was fleeing the nursing home. But the fact that he told me I *better go see him.*

He told me that he never wanted to see his dad again, well at the same time instantly worried about how he'd get haircuts. I see this as clear evidence that trying to suggest Joe's behaviors are ALL calculated types of bullshit…just aren't *true.*

CHAPTER EIGHT

"The splendor of a soul in grace is so seductive…that it surpasses the beauty of all created things." —Thomas Aquintas

I'm here to tell you that if that quote is true, it's good news. But have you noticed that in all the preceding chapters… I have fallen far short of whatever *mark* the quote suggests? Plus, the *inability* to face certain facts… seems to be an almost a *parallel theme* here with seeking the spiritual meaning of human existence.

It's true. People can get trapped in sterile, dependent relationships where a person just serves as an object for things like basic security. Then again, it is also possible to love out of strength rather than need. *Dear God, fill me with your perspective until I joyfully lay down my will for yours.*

Five months now since Joe moved out, and at least four months into his using again. He is broke, and I continue to try to find ways to get farther away from this scene. I feel compelled to get my own place as soon as possible because I believe that if he gets evicted, I will not be able to say, "No, you cannot come back here." It is the house his dad gave us.

The rent I am to pay his daughter gets less and less each month as I subtract out paying his truck insurance, cellphone coverage, the Menards bill minimum, and whatever he has borrowed from me recently. The month before, he said to *skip it altogether* as I'd also taken care of a lot of business details for him. This *now* he cannot remember. It is possible that his disease does not allow him to remember things correctly …*to protect his wounded pride.*

Who knows how he explains the *no rent check* to his daughter? But chances are good that he will have to say something bad about me…to try to save face.

I could tell by his phone call the previous Friday that he had reached a level of painful desperation. He told me he tried to pay me back some money the day before, that he rang my doorbell several times, and I wouldn't answer. I'm thinking I may have been blow drying my hair then because I did not hear him at all. Then he went into being totally disgusted with his family all around. I don't know if he meant his dad, kids and/or his sister... whom he tells me *he has plans to give an earful yet that day.*

Somewhere in his deluge of warbled statements, I hear him spew out how *I've cost him so much money it doesn't even matter anymore.* Where this came from and how he deduced it... I don't know. It doesn't really matter. His world is closing in fast. I can tell that his weekend will not be fun, and he is struggling mightily.

I decide to send a text to him on Sunday night...in an effort to try to see how bad off he is. This, I believe, will give me an idea about how fast I need to get somewhere else, as I have watched his addictions escalate to this point a couple of times already.

In this text to him now, I include a picture of a screwed-up garage door at a place I thought about looking at... asking if he thought it *looked too bad to fix.*

He texted me back right away. "You hurt my business so bad that I don't care I am not able to have friends that think of me as u do. You didn't pay raise room you think I'm such a piece of shit don't please don't contact me for that. Talk to your boyfriend I'm not your friend is nothing that you have that you like about me so please don't act like you do it unless you don't don't don't call me talk to me to dohh I can decipher don't please don't..."

I am welled up inside for the next 24 hours at least... as I picture him so emotionally burned that even a touch... would cause him to disintegrate.

The *"don't, don't, don't..."* so soft.

It came off like a child that has been scalded alive and can only just try to wrap themselves in their own brand of whatever protection they have available... to numb *enough* until the almost intolerable pain subsides.

A few days later, he calls me to let me know that he has sold this house I am living in. But then he tells me that he specifically chose which one of the rich guys he works for to sell it to... *based solely on who would let me stay here cheap if I wanted.*

I believe this to be the very sincere thing that it is. I *do* know that, regardless of the situation, he does as right by me as he can. Thus, I am back to doing frequent contact with him …calls about the house inspection details, etc.

He even asks to borrow a little cash…*since I know he's good for it… with the house selling,* etc. We make no mention of the foreboding text from the week before. He says his daughter's getting most of the money.

I still want to get my own house soon because I know the prices are about to really shoot up. Then one day, I'm cruising around trying to find the latest home that's caught my eye on the listings and I manage a whopping car accident. Suffice it to say that *trying to read the house information papers as you're going along…* makes it pretty easy to *run stop signs.*

*Suddenly…*I saw a car coming straight at me… seemingly out of nowhere. I tried to gas pedal it through the intersection as fast as I could, but the other car hit me really hard. My thigh crushed into the armrest on the driver's door, and it was just like an airbag had deplored. Instantly, my upper leg swelled to three times its size.

I stepped out of my car. It hurt to bear weight, but there were other things to deal with. I grabbed my cellphone to call 911. Yet, Joe's number popped up on the screen, so I hit that instead. He was there in minutes.

By this time… the ambulance people were trying to get me to go with them. I didn't want to. *I'm not sure who has to pay for this. I'm worried about how I'd get home from there… and on and on.*

Joe has made his way through the crowd of onlookers. He tells me to *go in the ambulance and get checked out…*and then I love him all over again because he gives me full eye contact and hear him softly saying, *"Remember you have artificial knees…you really have to get this all checked out ."* I hope I always do give him credit for the level of attention and *retention* he has paid to me over the years. Really! I am grateful for it, and I do appreciate it.

He handled the details… calling my boss and insurance company both right from the hospital emergency room. The x-rays came out okay, so I got to go …with my mammoth hematoma and a supply of pain pills. When he was settling me in at the house… his helper told me that he was just aghast when he first saw the accident scene. Joe came back that night to take me grocery shopping. The next morning, he took me to go get a rental car. Very, very wonderful. I got a couple good hugs in, too…*his* idea.

I had also been in the process of going on an overnight camping trip that weekend up north. He put the veto on taking my bike along. He did say too *he'd love to drive me* if he didn't have his boss in town. I let him know I really appreciated the gesture for sure.

As we were driving to go get the rental car, he blithers out that he *told Bergen he was helping me out.* I say nothing, and the conversation moves to something else. I assume he has decided to see if he is able to make her jealous, possibly as a measure of her affection for him? I base this on the mounting evidence that he is stuck at some early teenage level, emotionally. But even as I write this, I have to ask myself again…so what? Then… does that make him some kind of throw away person? No, it does not.

Last Thursday, I had a day off. I decide to run some errands. Upon return, I can see Joe's truck parked in front of my house from a half a block away. Since he moved out six months ago now, he has *always* called before he's come over, so this seemed really weird.

Then I see Joe and a girl coming down the front steps. Actually, I don't think he even realized it was me pulling up… probably not used to that rental car. I see him stammering to get some kind of statement out, but I cut in… greeting with a simple nod and then "Joe." Then I turn my attention to the gal, *and I know it is she.* "Bergen?" I say with enough questioning lilt in my tone that she nods back.

I see her hesitate about what she should do. She started to head for his truck. But I reach out my hand to offer to shake with her, and she does. I pause momentarily and say, "Wow, you remind me so much of one of his sisters. Wow, it's really…weird."

Meanwhile, Joe has come up with some other bullshit about bringing my BBQ grill back …and then something about getting his little flatbed trailer out of the alley. I just nod and make my exit into the house.

"In Life, sometimes getting hurt is a necessary path. Do not deny yourself of this experience, but never dwell in it. You have to go through it and not around it… for you to get over it." –Dodinsky

I try to get my bearings. I glance out into the yard and see that the grill is not back. This, at least, gives me enough gumption to go interact a little more. I touched up my lipstick, and out I go. They are kind of circling that flatbed trailer in the overgrown weeds as I approach.

I am guessing she'd have to be in her fifties, but she has a perfectly toned petite slender build, with beautiful long blonde hair swinging ever so delicately in a perfect ponytail. *Yes, it is the devil in a red dress, so to speak.* Although, sadly, I also think that he really left me…also *just* as much for the chance to rent a stainless steel kitchen to impress *anyone* he can with. I don't know if she would be considered a great beauty, but she's very appealing. Although, I see she is a smoker and possibly has a boob-job.

I lead off with "the grill doesn't *look* to be back" in my best *I know you are lying but I'm not going to make you eat the crow* tone.

Nervous little giggles all around. Joe tries to trump the bullshit in some stumble-bum way. So, I offer up a finish line. "I see…you just were deciding where to *put* the grill …should you *actually* bring it back."

Big roaring laughter then …and cleansing enough to cut the tension… plus…*kudos* to me…for offering up such a splendid tip to Bergen on how to *deal with his all-around low level of truth telling abilities.* I got the feeling they *both* even kind of understood that too.

I go *then* into complimenting Bergen on the beautiful hanging lamp she made him. She came back with compliments to me about the house being so really cool and creative, etc., *and it was sincere.* But I'm thinking, wow, so *he brought her over to show her the house.* I do have to say that we really did do something great here. It was a *dump,* and now it's an awesomely beautiful place to behold.

Joe was trying to find a way to cut the lock off the cable around his flatbed trailer, so I took Bergen on my own version of a tour. Suddenly, I am just actually thrilled to be having a conversation with another artist whose caliber

I admire.

I decide on the spur of that moment to turn it into an opportunity for a long overdue explanation of how some of his late step mother's broken and excess jewelry ended up in an art project/room divider I was working on in my basement pseudo studio.

First, I point out to her the privacy fence Joe put up. It flows effortlessly over the dips and curves of the yard, blending in with the house perfectly. I *then* show her how, *looking over the top of it,* you can see both of the next two houses have serious roof problems. The eaves of the house closest sag down, and the house just past that has a weird crookedness going on.

She seems to totally see my point and agrees in a manner liken to: *yes, it is a significant factor in the big picture! It should be dealt with!* At least in my head anyway, and believe me, I'd been waiting something like a year now to *get vindication* on that point. Joe was hideous to me when I tried to explain to him that we could try to cover that deficit somehow. He said *"shut the fuck up"* to me … in front of another AA guy.

I was so embarrassed for him. *I knew then, at six months sober, he was, at best, still operating only as a dry drunk. Comments like that were just announcing that fact to the whole world… with only him not seeing it.*

What Bergen *actually* responded with was "I do see… and believe me, I'm a perfectionist." *This too I store for later material /information to mull over.*

I go on to explain that I had thought about using some of the old jewelry for a fence *topping* project. This then also being a sort of tribute to her, as she had lived there thirty plus years. I noticed Bergen nodding like she was affirming it as wonderfully novel. When I got that idea, I know I mentioned to Joe that *I might try a tribute* … without saying what exactly.

Anyway, I blither out that *I'm thinking Joe is mad at me…*because the jewelry… in the end …turned up on a room divider project *that I was probably going to take with me, and I'm not part of the family or whatever, even though it* was stuff he gave me when we were sorting through it in the first place, combined with my own stuff. The truth is…*when I found out the house was just going to be turned into a rental,* I decided, "Fuck-it."

Granted, this was a long-convoluted monologue, but right at *I think Joe might be mad at me,* I saw her do a shake of disagreement. That registered with me. Anyway, I'm sure we both could have gone on a lot longer with art project talk too, but Joe interrupted with *"time to go… things to do."*

Also…I was aware that he was buzzed up. God only knows on what exactly. I'd recently found his favorite De-Walt drill bit… that he had converted into a one hitter… in my old recliner, and he was happy to take it. But at least it's easier to maintain a semi normal lifestyle doing pot… than alcohol…possibly *slowing down* his catapulting into oblivion somewhat.

ANYWAY, as they were leaving, everything was on such a stonily, friendly basis. He gushes out a warm, *"Good-bye, and you know I love you."* He says it *without* reservation, and it's easy for me to read his implied attitude as: "See… I can say this right in front of Bergen. *Here,* I am allowed to love whoever I want, guilt-free, *and call it love to boot!"*

He says "I love you" *again*… with the end tone suggesting that I am to respond in kind.

"Yeah," I say with no hint of *anything*. I turn to go into the house.

The next day, he came over for something. I can't remember *what* now. But he nervously, yet softly said, "By the way… thanks for being so nice to Bergen yesterday."

"I just feel so sorry for her" rolls out of my mouth. And *unusual* for me… it wasn't rehearsed in any way up ahead… at least not consciously.

But then his "we don't have that kind of relationship" comeback, in retrospect, *was not* a very smooth flow to what I'd just said to him. Thus, I have now concluded that the whole point of him commenting about it in the first place was to get that piece of information out to me.

I am fully aware that *an addict, one active in his addiction,* cannot actually *love* anyone. So there really is no point in who loves who here. But I have had time to process now, and I find I am able to do it without the pain, fear, and constant obsession of it.

Joe is fun to be around in his *up* time… no doubt about it… a laugh a minute.

He does full scale cooking show-styled dialoguing as he cooks… on and on. He hams it up and hams it up. God knows working in a nursing home would almost require capitalizing on every perk you could get some days. He *is* charming.

Yet, throughout this deep and in-depth emotional affair, he has been carrying on with her, he has done the side whoring thing too. Again, he did say he was a sex addict. I'm sure there are many facets to this. I believe she is a decent person and probably even God fearing.

Then, my *new* landlord sent Joe's partner over here to change the locks. He told me that Joe's drinking during the day is really getting bad. He is in the fierce gripe of a horrible monster, and I am glad I do not to have to watch this *up close* again. I've even told him that.

Basically, it comes down to meeting people where they're at. I can interact in humility. I can admit that I struggle mightily still with a few of *my* addictions. But then with God's help…I *need* to conquer them! Modeling this is what I can and must do… in ways that do not shame. I know he is sick and suffering horribly with this disease of alcoholism… fully activated. I will pray for his recovery and that I may be a help in whatever way the holy spirit leads to do.

Dear God,

I see that I do trust in you completely now, and that is so awesome. I feel like for the most part, my negative emotions here have subsided. I feel a sense of calmness in my spirit, and I know that is you… speaking to me. I am happy to be gathering the strength to do whatever it is you would ask of me. I pray that I not become distracted from the work you have planned for me.

And I thank you for allowing me such an avenue to share the pain that I have been through so that the experience will not have been wasted. May I continue to do your will, always.

Yet…I once again ditch my 12 -step overeating program. As an addict, I am *defiant* by nature. My eating is probably even worse than his drinking truth be told. I still get all caught up in the rationalizing. I heard about some other people having great success with an all veggies and protein diet, and I decide to spend *tons* of money trying that. But I cannot maintain it. So then I decide to check out a new church-program that teaches sugar in moderation. I don't make it one day, and I'm binge eating all the sugar foods I can find.

By the time I get a follow-up call from that church, I had another ten pounds on at least. I explain to this guy that I am a critical level food addict. It has been a lifelong problem. He tells me *so- be- it. Then I do need to find a program designed specifically for my level of addiction, and sorry, but they aren't it.* But he does call back and pray for me too.

In fact, the area where Joe and I do *match* the closest is in our level of addiction… okay and *our tempers.* The only real hope for me at all …is a very structured and rigid intervention. The only plan that does this is the tightest branch they offer of overeaters anonymous. And I need to understand that at least part of God's will for me, more than likely, is to model recovery for people that have struggled with addiction since childhood. I've worked this program on and off for years. A big part of my moving down here was to be near the thriving hub of it. But *I've spit it back out quite a few times anyway for no real good reason either.*

I pray I finally do grasp it as the freedom it is to live my life to the fullest. I know that the 12-step program was designed specifically for *hard-core addiction.* It is the medication for what is wrong with me mentally, and total sugar abstinence is the answer for me physically. Working it is the only way to health and joy for me. Already I have become aware that my Higher Power has delivered me into a state now where I am very happy to unleash this power in my life.

Joe ended up with only a very little left from selling the house. I suspect that he was over generous and gave way too much of it… to his daughter.

He did then bring $2000.00's in cash to me. Even if I have to write off the rest of it, he has tried to look after me the best he can. I have gotten by very well…just by being able to live here so cheap. At this point, it would just be a bonus.

I also really wanted to try to get him to do a change of responsibility on his phone bill and off of mine. I wait well over a week to find out if any progress is being made in these areas. I wait a few more days and then go over to his house… before I think he'll leave for work. I knock and call him at the same time, over and over. He yells through the door that he's not even up yet.

But then he calls me. I let him know that not returning my calls is the number one basic offense here. For that, he does genuinely apologize. I love when he does this by the way. He promises he will jump in the shower and deal with it within the hour. … He'll come by and see me.

"You don't need to come over," I say as I get in my car to go. "Just call them and get it done, please." Soon, I do get a call from the phone company telling me he is on the other line trying to do this, and yes, I give my permission. While I'm at it though, I talk with another representative there enough to realize that this is not going to pan out. They are checking Joe's credit, and it's not going to fly.

I do press him for more details.

"Where's the truck situation these days?"

"When are you going to get a checking account open?"

"Did you actually pay off that child support bill?"

He responded as upfront as anyone could be…*the money from selling the house didn't go too far. Notice the only extra bill he could squeeze in was what he could do for me. So please don't think I'm not a priority.*

I am softening up by then, but I still slide in "God you're such a *major liability in my life*… I'm scared I'll miss getting a decent house."

But bless his heart. His calm answer back to me was, "Jolene, you know that whatever house you get…ultimately… is in God's hands." And I do know it. Plus, this came out of him so automatically that I know he's spent some time thinking about my situation in general.

Then, he told me he has quit drinking. "Really, I might as well just go jump off a bridge as do that; it's so dangerous for me." I could tell by the tone of his voice that he was straight. Sadly though, I've never even heard of anyone at his level of addiction to come out of it by themselves. So, I very much doubt it will last.

Still… *thank you, Jesus,* just rolls out of me when I hear him say things like that, and I tell him I've gone back to my very structured program for food addiction myself. "I'm not even going to pretend that I know how to operate without the higher power at the helm. I surrender."

He mummers an additional *I'm with you there* and goes on to tell me quite a lot of *just between you and me, I'm really broke* stuff.

I have known since that Easter morning I stopped by his place and saw the 50 some Real Estate: *Get Rich Quick* kind of CD's he'd spent his last $3000 on… that he was in a slide he wasn't going to pull out of, and I think that's when he first really knew it too.

But that's part of the *carrot wagging* of this disease. Every day, he'd probably buzz up one way or another and get to a level of enough false reality to *just hang on…* some days a little higher than others… to protect his ego. He went on to tell me that *he's been lining up his own work.* He's been very busy, *but he's depressed.* I bet he is. I don't see how he can continue to maintain.

I do again run the idea by him to *maybe check into the hospital for a day and at least try to get on an anti-depressant.* All in all, it was a great call… because it was *honest.* God knows I love him, but he is just going to have to find his own way.

I did my *own budget review,* and I see that maybe I should just stay right where I'm at until I get my last two classes done… to get my Master's degree. Then, I should be able to look for an income increase. Otherwise, the money will be too tight …if I get a bigger payment.

Of course, I am tempted to think about doing a live together deal again with Joe, but… I've been around that *compromising* mountain already, and it doesn't work. I am not going to live with a guy that I'm not married to. It is just plain not in God's will. I have a feeling that this is my big test now.

I pray and then do the next best thing. I try not to get ahead of myself. I am *content with what I do have, which is a pretty good set-up…thanks to Joe.* But I now realize that in order to recover… I need to let go of my thinking and truly enter the spiritual world. It is here that I can embrace the serious business of becoming a confident adult human being and *believe that successful partnering is about two people who are really able to see that the problems… lie in themselves.*

"All true creativity (in relationships too) begins with
a tranquility deep inside us. So first we need to find that "serenity."
Then enjoy that personal solitude for a time until, finally, we are in
a position to ignite our passion and reach out to change the world around us.
-RUMI

CHAPTER NINE

"God turns you from one feeling to another and teaches by means of opposites so that you will have two wings to fly, not one."—Rumi

When I talked with Joe a few weeks back, *and he admitted that he was depressed,* I dropped *my latest assortment of treatment- facility-literature* in his mail box. Then in the next conversation about his losing phone, I went right ahead with *"why don't you get some help?"*

Joe's *"there is no help for guys like me..."* were just about the saddest words I've ever heard.

"Yes, there is! Teen Challenge for Adults takes people without insurance. I put the information in your mailbox."

"Oh, why don't you go to treatment?" *Click.*

I decide to leave well enough alone for now. I have enough to deal with. I have just learned that I am being *terminated without benefits.* Mostly unjustly and maybe the union can prove it... but it will take months if not years to work through it. I do not share this information with Joe because ...what would be the point? I don't really need sympathy. I need to pull out of it, head held high. I sent him a text the first week with just: *"Are you doing all right?"*

He answered back right away *that he was working out of town to make some fast bucks and would call soon.*

I spend at least the first ten days after being fired jumping all the hoops to get my meager retirement coming and filling out every job application I can find, hoping to get some benefits. I do believe it is in God's hands, and I mostly am holding up. But I also know that the pain pills from my accident are working as a crutch. I need to shake them too.

I go to a church service. I feel such shoulder pain that I am convinced that God is *squeezing* me into believing I could have a heart attack if I don't dump all the pain pills into a toilet right away…so I do.

I pick up eating extra food again to offset the *no pain pills*…binging all night on what was in the house that seemed yummy…plain yogurt with cherries and grape nuts, times 3-4 bowls full. Then up and dressed this morning to go through Mc-Donald's and then to the grocery store for three do-nuts, a bag of M&M's and a bag of chips… and a chocolate frosted Rice Krispy treat… in case I never have another chance at them either… .*all binges being the last one and all.*

I have *at least* decided that I will be attending overeater's anonymous meeting by that evening. I cannot afford to binge like this for any length of time. What clothes I do have *that fit* won't even work in a week at this rate. I will also have to find another sponsor, as the one I have cannot continue with me after three slips, and *I just got there*. But I do have to stop.

*****

I decide to calm myself with some phlein-air *writing*. My senses are engaged. It is a beautiful fall day. I am comfortably stationed on a chaise lounge in my backyard. I have a good strong cup of coffee next to me on an outdoor side table I hand painted. A few bumblebees are making their way through the bushes in my foreground. My backdrop is the beloved upper level of the backyard we were able to so wondrously fashion …mostly from scraps. Joe's old tool collection is still displayed beautifully on the rustic shed.

I am remembering that what I really liked the most about the big painted saw Joe brought home from some yard sale was that the artist signed it *with a love- note* on the back. It is a labor of love, and that makes it great.

Regardless of the bullshit way everything went down, Joe has made a conscious effort to make sure that I am okay. I am happy to have such a beautiful yard to operate from.

Never say never, I guess. I gave in to the urge and called him because I thought if he really was doing a big job and he knew I'd lost my mine… chances were …he *would* try to repay some of the money he owed me. He is gallant in this respect. Sometimes, it's like he feels almost overwhelmed to give … when he believes someone is really needy… Here I catch myself mentally renaming this book, "Joe Robin-hood."

I call. He answers. I tell him my big bad and shocking news. Joe is beyond control in his contempt, outrage, shock, sadness, and caring about the unfairness of my termination. I have had enough time to process it. I am ready to *just find another job.*

He cannot accept it, and quite frankly… no one else on this earth is as aware as he is …of the ridiculous crap I did endure on this job. In fact, *he needs to be consoled from me* that I will be okay. Then…I think because my news is so harsh… he feels comfortable enough to own up to *his* sad news.

"Well… guess what happened to me," he says. "You think that's bad… the IRS pounded on my door one morning and said I owed $750,000's in back taxes… and they confiscated almost everything I own. They even took my computer." He sketched in a few more details, but suddenly, I realized regardless of what actually happened, *he had been living out of his truck for the last couple of weeks.*

He went on. More stories about how his account had been frozen. Bergen's birthday was such a mess… *they were done.* He was still doing some good jobs. But somewhere in there …he mentioned *jumping off a bridge again* too. He did end the call with *repeated I love you's …and how he'd get me some good money soon.* We'd go to breakfast in the morning.

But…he didn't even text until the next afternoon…said he was doing a paint job. Then he called that night to say we'd go at 7am the next morning… meet him there. He'd bring me $2,000's. Then, *three* sets at least of the "I love you, and I hope you know it. Do you? Do you really know it?"

"I do."

I knew there was a better chance that he *wouldn't* show. I know he thinks telling people what he thinks they most want to hear… is the best gift he can give. That was over a week ago now. No one heard from him for days. It wasn't that hard to figure out that he was just plain too broke to keep up his lifestyle.

I'm guessing he probably had to break his lease six months early, and God only knows how far behind he was on utilities. He probably sold his stuff for enough to get by for a while and to try to at least clean it out nice enough that the landlord would forgive him somewhat.

It's funny now that I think about it. Just a few weeks before this, he happened to mention to me that I *was better with money than he was.* Anyway, he did answer my call a few days later. He was mad because his sister wouldn't borrow him money for an efficiency apartment. He is still so upset about *my job situation*; he would still cry to even talk about it.

I let him know that I really didn't expect any money from him at this point, all things considered...but I do expect him to answer his phone. He apologized. *He will never do that again.* Then so many more convoluted stories, I can't even track them all now. He was going to bring me the dog on Thursday night because it wasn't fair to keep him in the truck all day, then that changed to 6am on Friday morning. Now, its Sunday night... no dog, no calls, no returned text.

I don't *know* where he is. In one of our last phone conversations, I was at least able to remind him that *he has a disease and that maybe he should forgive himself.* Also, to reiterate that some of the long term treatment programs do have financial planning programs, etc. He is not as terminally unique as he thinks he is. These are common problems.

"*Maybe*" did come out of him at one point, but then he worked it around to telling me that *he has not been drinking night and day... like I think.* I countered that *it was his ego that was so out of control.*

He said it was *his pride.*

Same difference... I don't think he got the point. The thing is that *what* and *exactly how often a person uses* is not the issue *as much as why.* The reasons behind what ends up constituting possibly even a *lifetime* of restless, irritable, and discontent feelings are what we need to deal with.

The last recovery movie I saw talked a great deal about learning how to really *help* addicts... instead of just forcing them into a life of crime. So okay, I hope some of this is useful to someone, somewhere.

Then my hot water heater went out. The repair men that came over had worked with Joe up until recently. They wanted to know what I knew about where he may be. *Long gone,* I say. *He's using crack,* they say, *buying and selling.* Obviously, not so slickly, I think, since he ended up so broke. Wow, it rips at my heart…I will stop right now and compose a letter to him:

> Dear Joe,
>
> I do want to thank you for all the things you did for me long after what could be called the honeymoon phase. Somehow, you did make sure I ended up with a comfortable place to live.
>
> I want to thank you for putting a big closet in my bedroom and a coat closet in the entryway. Thanks for putting such a fabulous roof over my head, a shower in the house, putting in a bigger vanity, a new deck out front, a great privacy fence in the backyard, switching out the appliances, putting up the cupboards, and hooking up for a dryer.
>
> Plus, one of my fondest memories was the day I came back from up north with a lot of plants and you just dropped what you were doing and dug out all the sod for me to plant the stuff. Man, I love you.
>
> I am honored that you made sure I had a sturdy new floor in the camper. I love the shingles you put on it, and thank you so much for the impetus to wood-grain it. I know it turned out so much better because you cared about it too.
>
> Really, thanks for even cutting the backboards for my art projects too, by the way. Plus, I remember how hard you tried to find my art show a few years back even though you were in the throes of excess drinking issues.

I am so grateful for all the times that you listened to my tales of woe about work. Right up to last week when you told me you'd take a bullet in the heart on the steps of the capital for the injustice they did to me. I am so proud to know you.

I love that you called my clients on their birthdays when you knew no one else would. I remember so many times when you even cried with me. I do love you.

From the bottom of my heart, I want you to know that I appreciate how hard you did in fact try to warn me that it could turn out this way. Even though I still want to believe it is a condition that can be in remission with the right God directed treatment plan…

I can love you from a far for now…you are not pure poison. My job is to model the *true fullness* of a spiritual life.

Not this hovering around *pseudo recovery bullshit* I have been stuck in for years now.

-Love with all my heart,

Jolene

The shame-based aspect of addiction is worth a good look again, too, because it has all too often been written off with *labeling* tendencies. Some addicts are *seen as* just plain psychopathic, for example. But a true psychopath *does* not have a conscience. So, I do want to throw out a couple more little stories for you.

When Joe's dad was still trying to live in a semi-independent apartment, we decided to help him get set-up for a little exercise bike riding. We went to Menards to get a handle for him to grab onto, making his dismount that much smoother. The only ones they had were so expensive; it was unreal. As we stood there debating it, Joe just said, *"Oh hell, it's for my Dad,"* and he got it. This, by the way, the same Dad that made Joe feel so unworthy… so many times.

I remember a few years ago, he'd been doing some construction work and wanted to put some stuff in a dumpster parked nearby. First though, he thought he should knock on that person's door and let them know. It turned out to be a very nice older woman that lived there. They got to talking. He learned she had made floral arrangements for years, *out of plastic.* Now she had tons of them sitting around and didn't know what to do with them. So that night, he brought me over to take some pictures, etc., to see if I had any ideas for her.

*****

Anyway, now I've read books where they are suggesting people's brain chemicals could be altered by the experience of this type of relationship. Joe did emotionally hurt me. I hurt him emotionally, accidently too. But *true also* is that we *did* need each other for almost basic survival, and we *did* provide that for each other in our best haphazard fashion, considering the afflictions we suffer from.

However, I have trusted God all along that *going in for a close look was not going to destroy me.* I've heard it said that "Just the right amount of introspection can bring about all sorts of wisdom and creativity." And again, I thank God for the gift of art…as I use it to rewire my neutrons. I was able to stay busy concentrating on projects and *being in the now.* This did stop intrusive thoughts from pulling up those strong feelings to the point where they paralyzed me. It helped me rebuild my inner quiet and wisdom and compassion enough to remember he's a person with an illness.

I will continue to pray for Joe. I hope that he never ends up classified like a complete psychopath. That is why we need to find a way to reach people like this before it is too late. I believe that the 12 steps were founded on Godly principles, and that is where I stand firm. Therefore, I must continue to work my program in that I will pray to be Holy Spirit lead in every situation.

Joe is missing. No one knows where he is. I am concerned, but I am not going to go looking for him. He doesn't want to be found. I will pray that he truly does find God's purpose for his life. Today… I will make every effort to just let God deal with him.

God wants me to develop *my* gifts and achieve *my* purpose in life. I've survived hard financial times… with an attitude of gratitude. *What could be horrendous stumbling blocks can also be turned into stepping stones.* If I am willing to have God remove my shortcomings, He will do it His way. The same is true for every situation in my life.

Then, at 6am *a few weeks later,* my doorbell buzzes. There stands Joe with the dog and a big bag of dog food. I let him in. He gives me a hug and a kiss. I am glad to see him, but I feel stiff. Joe gives me the dog. He tries to reassure me that he will be alright. Off he goes then… to stay with a buddy he's working with.

A week after that, Joe stops by. He gives me his new phone number. He shows me he has an $800 check to cash, and he said he'd bring me some money. I needed to go to the library to get my work done for an online class…so he left.

Joe calls then early on a Saturday morning… *to tell me he's in Chicago.* He shares some details. *He'd received 150 text messages from Bergen when he went missing a few weeks back… telling him she loved him…for him to come back…so he did come back and pick up that job. Then when he'd left my house a few nights back…he drank and went to her place. She woke him up at 3 in the morning, telling him he had to go. He was mad. She called the cops, etc. He took off driving.*

He went on to tell me she was *a spoiled little Daddy's girl,* etc. When he started the *I was the best woman he'd ever known…* I took the opportunity to tell him… *it was wrong for us to ever live together…I'd take my share of the fault in it…and that I'd never do that again.* This point now driven home for good, I hope.

*He sounded really rough…*coughing and coughing. *Then…* he told me he talked to the counselor from the treatment center I'd arranged to call him. He said now he had decided to come back and go into the long-term program. *Could I download the application for him?*

I am already on my third verse of *Thank-you Jesus* before I ask *how* he's going to get back here.

"Well… that's a problem," he says, *"…I'm broke."*

I don't want him to rob somebody or something…so I tell him I will wire him some money…*which I don't know how to do.* Because he wanted to be as considerate as possible, he insisted that I continue on to the 12-step meeting I had planned to attend that morning. Afterwards, I can call, and we can figure out the where and when of it. I put my phone on silent for the meeting and forgot that I did that. Then when I called to square up the plan…we decide to do the money wiring from a Walmart. I am always flustered when I am in a situation I am not familiar with…so it took a long time to find a Walmart. Then when I did finally get the money wired…I called and told him it was on its way. He said *good because his phone was about to die too.*

I took off and dinked around shopping, etc., on my way home. *Finally*, I realized that my cellphone was vibrating in my purse. Wow, I forgot it was on silent. Joe had been trying to call that whole time to let me know he needed the processing numbers from me. Thankfully, I did have the receipt, and I was able to give them to him… standing there almost dead trying to call for maybe even an hour. So, shit… I felt horrible.

A couple more days go by. I call him. He tells me the *transmission went out on his truck (supposedly only 3-4 hours away now). He can't decide what to do… but a nice farmer is helping him.* Every day then…I call and check in. We have lovely pleasant chats. He tells me he landed a good paint job there to pay for a transmission, etc.

Almost 2 weeks after I wired him that money, I learn from his sister in town that he talked to his dad on Bergen's phone. He went the opposite direction. He is now 4 states away.

I have had it. My chest cramped up. I tried to lie down to feel better. It didn't work. I got up and went for a drive. It felt so tight…I couldn't even breathe. I knew what I had to do. I reached for the necklace. *A circle's round and has no end; that's how long I want to be your friend.* I pulled as hard as I could, and it broke. I did it fast… because I didn't want to give myself a chance to reconsider. I flung the pieces out the window and sped away, and I could breathe again. It's good to know that *I am capable* of breaking it off… if I have to.

I sent him a text: "When I think about how giving you money has deterred you from reaching your true bottom…that's when I feel the worst."

*****

CHAPTER TEN

"Dwell in Me and I will dwell in you.
Just as no branch can bear fruit of itself without abiding
(being vitally united to) the vine, neither can you bear
fruit unless you abide in me."
—John 15:4

I am doing pretty well at accepting myself these days. I'm starting to like my morning mirror talks. I see that I exemplify a shabby chic style of presenting my made-up face to the world. Yes, it's a little messy, but this *not to the point of perfection...* sets well with me. I find that I actually don't mind a few unruly eyebrow hairs. I am happy to learn that a common suggested prayer to understand God's will is to ask God to *increase my desire if something is right for me and to decrease my desire... if it is not.*

Shortly after his fleeing in early November, *we all lost contact with Joe.* The last phone number for him went straight into the message: "The person you are trying to contact is not accepting calls right now." No one in his family even heard from him over Christmas.

The first Sunday in January, Joe was heavy on my mind, and it was constant. *But it wasn't like earlier foreboding feelings where I could conjure up even what his carcass could look like in a ditch somewhere, thankfully.* I even found myself sewing a neat little curtain to put on the bathroom cabinet that Joe used to complain *looked so cluttered.* I went to church. I prayed to understand this *feeling his presence so deeply* again. I came up only with the simple truth again, that contradictions do co-exist in people.

My phone rang at 7:50 pm, and I didn't recognize the area code.

"Hello?"

"Is Jolene there?" comes at me in a muffled voice.

"Yes, this is her."

"Do you know who this is?"

"Yes." Just rolls out of me automatically… even though his voice was so graveled. "YES! OH MY GOD, YES! How are you?"

"I'm still alive…I'm still alive."

"Where are you?"

"I'm in Texas, working with some Mexicans painting cabinetry for a rich guy. He's an artist and boy is he *out there*…but he's nice."

"Well, how *are* you?"

"Well, I ain't gonna lie to you. It's been rough. I just now finally got into a house with four other Mexican guys and an older lady that only speaks Spanish… who cooks for us beans simmered in fat mostly…but it's not too bad. I'm working a good job now for $22 .50 an hour. God is taking care of me throughout all of this though. Remember the chain store I used to manage?"

"Yes."

"Well, I had a framed photo in my truck of the store opening and the manager of the store down here decided that was a good enough reason to let me stay in that parking lot for 12 weeks I've picked cans and tried to even do some mechanic work… and now finally doing ok. How are you?"

I tell him the highlights. I am getting by with a low paying part-time job… but enough to get by with my meager retirement check until I can get something better. He asks how my leg is now from the car accident… how my Mom's doing and that cousin I'm a guardian for… my daughter and her sick Dad…*all before he asks about the dog*. When he gets to this, I just have to take a deep breath.

"Well………I don't have the dog anymore."

I hear the "What?" in such a shocked and puzzled tone that I can see the knit forming in his brow.

"Ya… the new landlord said I couldn't have a pitbull because his insurance wouldn't cover it. I tried to explain that we had run into that ourselves, and found out that State Farm will. He told me that might be so, but there was no way he was about to change his insurance company for the 50 some rentals he owns…the dog has to go." I pleaded how *he means something to me… and to Joe…that I'd need at least a week to find a good home for him.* I ended up putting a write-up on Craigslist and filtered through the responders until I found a great family for him. *I would have loved to have had a conversation with you about it. I called and called… and no answer."*

"Ya," he says, "I threw that last cheap phone …to stop Bergen from calling me. I'm *so done* with her. I loved her, but I love you more… I'm realizing."

I say nothing.

"I'm borrowing my roommate's phone for this call. I plan to get the screen fixed on my good one next paycheck."

"Well, anyway… I brought the dog to Grandma's house at Thanksgiving. I went to my Brother's for a while, and when I came back, he was sitting on Gramma's lap eating apples."

I hear and then join in his hearty laugh, *resonating like parents chuckling over their adorable child.* "So at least from that… I knew he was ready to branch out and trust other people."

"Ya… I guess."

I let him know that his Dad told me at Christmas time *not to worry because at least you do have a good trade,* and I could hear the gulp in his voice. Evidently, it registered that his Dad was stating *a positive thing about him.*

He brought up the last text I'd sent him. He went into how *the thing is that he always disappoints.* I know he feels such shame, but he doesn't have to. If only somehow, some-way, he could really completely surrender to a support system and wrap himself around the 12-step programming … life as he knows it would quantum leap into awesome. But I don't need to play God here. I can listen, but no more money for sure.

We talked for over an hour. He said he told some guy he's working for a .bout me… artist stuff. *He thinks about me everyday; I've always been his best friend.* I could tell he wasn't coming around to any kind of thinking about treatment, and I didn't go there. I didn't want to scare him off.

Then I listened to him tell me again about how he was planning a fantastical nationwide walk…a meeting set up in April now with Good Morning America… to elaborate on his interviewing the homeless, etc… that he felt it was God's will for him to do this. Who am I to argue? Even though I doubt he really understands why he himself is now homeless, is he aware that many people are homeless just because they did run off and now have no proof of residence for a county to provide them benefits?

"Yep," he said, "who knows, maybe I'll even make it big… and someday we can live high on the hog…I've got to try… and if it doesn't work… oh well…I tried." I demurred on the highlife, but let him go on. I tell him a few more updates. He mentions he shouldn't be using up all the guy's minutes and then tells me more stories, and I tell him some more.

Finally, I tell him it's just so great to know he's OK. *But don't be thinking I've been pining over him. (No, I shouldn't,* he says). He tells me he loves me. I tell him I will always love him. And I probably will because underneath this lost and scared little boy of an addict… lies a really decent person.

> *"They say love is blind, I disagree. Infatuation is blind; love is all-seeing and accepting.*
>
> *Love is seeing all the flaws and blemishes and accepting them. Love is accepting the bad habits and mannerisms, and working around them. Love is recognizing all the fears and insecurities, and knowing your role is to comfort. Love is working through all the challenges and painful times.*
>
> *Infatuation is fragile and will shatter when life is not perfect. Love is strong and it strengthens because it is real."*
>
> *-Author unknown*

Late in January of this cold and unrelenting winter, my phone rang around 8pm. It was a police station not too far away. They had found our dog …hit by a car along the road…*dead.* When I heard those words, my first thought was that Joe must never know…that it would be too painful. I listened to the details. They couldn't figure out where the dog lived so they traced him to me through his chip.

I told them I only had an e-mail address for the people I had given him to. I told them I'd try to get ahold of them that way. The officer was kind enough to take the body to a freezer at the station for a few days until I could decide what to do.

I got off the phone. I was so sad. My daughter, bless her sensitive soul, posted the most excellent words on Facebook for me:

> *"A good dog never dies. He always stays. He walks beside*
> *you on a crisp autumn day when frost is on the fields and*
> *winter's drawing near; his head is within your hand in*
> *his old way."*
>
> *- Author unknown*

"I'm so sorry for your loss mom! He was a good boy!"

Ya… I'm bawling. That dog taught me so much about the attitude of forgiveness. I'd like to think it was *all* "no matter what life brings you, kick some grass over that shit and move on." I never heard anything back from the people that had him last.

I decided to get a freezer and keep him in my basement until I can do a proper burial for him in the spring. Plus, it just seemed fitting to bury him here in this backyard where he spent most of his life… under the herbs in the flower bed in front of the beautiful mural I painted on the back-retaining wall.

Suddenly, without forethought, I just up and hit the number on my phone for Joe's roommate. I asked him to have Joe call me. Low and behold, he did call right back.

"You called?" … in this huskier tone, now *sounding so set in.*

I tried to tell him what happened in a matter of fact way. I would say almost a *deadpan* delivery because it was… but the pun is not funny.

"He must have run away… I should have kept him with me."

I replied vaguely. "We'll never really know what happened, but I can't just let them *throw the body in a heap somewhere!"*

"No," concurring on that. But then, he went off on a spiel about how *I will have to do… what I feel I have to do.* From there, he went into a ditty about how *well he left me sitting rent-wise, etc.* Who knows? Maybe he was feeling horrible now… *also* because he didn't have any way to help out…*and how against his grain that is.*

"This is *not* about money…I need to know what you think I should do here. It's really not even legal to bury an animal in city limits… I just feel really, really bad."

His responding "I do too…" *did* then fully reveal his pain.

From that point in the conversation, he did talk nicer… *he'd try to send some money to help buy the freezer, and he'd call in a few days.*

Even though the dog was frozen when I picked him up to bring him home, it *was* good to feel him. That poet was right. *His head was in my hand in the old way.* He was a good boy.

When my phone rang a few days after that, I saw that it was from the phone Joe borrows from his roommate. I pleasantly projected, "Hello." I was surprised to hear such a thick Mexican accent until I realized it was the room-mate himself on the line. *I learn that Joe had disappeared again.* This roommate tells me *how much he liked him because he's such a nice guy.*

That he was sad to find him gone. Do I know where he is … and if he is alright? I do *not* know, and *again*, there is now no way to get ahold of him.

✲✲✲✲✲

I was happy that I did homework this week on Step 12.

"It is common to feel a little off sometimes in our 12th Step experiences, but I will find later they are mere stepping stones to better things. Maybe my heart has been set on getting someone in particular sobered up, and they relapse successively. Or…even the reverse can happen where I get highly elevated due to success… and I get too possessive of some newcomer. I could start

giving advice I'm not competent to give, and it's rejected or there's more confusion. I may be tempted to overmanage things, and I get rebuffed, etc. But these are all really only the pains of growing up."

I know that even as I falter in my journey through life, God is never going to let go of my hand. I am now on the lookout for all that God is doing in my life. I have not lost sight of the influences of those around me. Al-anon does teach that completely giving up on someone is always a personal decision that no one else can make for us. We all have to find our own answers. Mine are learning good boundaries for starters, I know. The balance lies in learning how to take care of myself physically, financially, and emotionally.

Sunday night halfway into March now, my phone again rings with an unknown number.

"Hey!"

My happy "Hey" right back to him… falls in like I'd talked to him this morning.

He laughs, knowing I knew it was him… instantly.

"Where are you?" seems like a pretty good lead off.

"Nashville, Tennessee…working for a big commercial painting company."

"Well, how are you? You're sounding good much better than the last time I talked to you."

"Good, good…working seven days a week sometimes…keeps me out of trouble. Living with Mexicans again for a $100's a month…doing ok."

"Well, I've been worried about you… and so has your old roommate, Peppy. He's called a few times now."

"You know not to worry about me. I'm a survivor."

"Well, believe me, I've got *hedge of protection* in every prayer for you." I fill him in on the general news and tell him that his daughter has been trying to find him now too.

He was his wonderful compassionate self. Still, I point blank asked him *why he called.*

He tells me he just finally now got a phone and then meanders around a bit… only to land firmly on his "I am so done with Bergen" line.

"I don't want to talk about her. She doesn't have anything to do with this. Really, I don't believe you've been faithful to any women *ever*." I delivered this pretty calmly… considering it's been in the back of our relationship all along.

Joe is really taken back and choked up when he tells me *that's not true. That he did love his wife, and when she divorced him, he went off the deep-end and has just been an idiot or some such thing… ever since.*

"Well, that may be true, but the point is not what or who or how or why, it's that you need help. *Period.*" I just stay matter of fact in tone, and I don't push it. I can hear him agreeing as I go.

Then, rather impulsively, I find myself telling him about getting in a fight with his dad.

"When I went out to your Dad's the last time to tell him that you'd called and you were OK, he started this whole deal about *what was wrong with me… for even caring that you were alright.* So, I got mad and told him to "just go to sleep and leave.""

"Well, don't feel bad about that. It's who he is. He walked out on all of us kids when we were little, so I seriously doubt he knows what unconditional love is. You love me unconditionally, and that's not something he can understand."

"Yeah… well… I'm not going back out to see him for a while…You really need to call your daughter now that's she's reaching out."

"Ya, I'm gonna." I hear him choking up again… *how much he loves her.* Then *how much he loves me…* and I can't remember all exactly. I did close with "I love you too."

Evidently, he's toned it down, which works for a while. Switching it up with some combination of overwork, pull-tabs, watching TV, maybe some weed, a little daily drinking, and actin' like a *player…* whatever makes him feel *temporarily* good enough to not have to actually *drown* his sorrows. Addicts usually do have more than one substance use disorder. It is a sort of culture of addiction they immerse themselves in and can't find their way out of.

Joe told me that his new boss *just loves* him. Well, everyone loves him…at least for a while. He is the classic version of the *salesman extraordinaire* typified in the Big Book. But I know *his restless, irritable and discontent-ness* will cause him to act out in some form or another without the help he needs. I am sad about this because he is better than just functioning in his dysfunction.

That said, I also do *not* want to discount really understanding this disease. Some secular researchers even believe that addicts have so much trouble staying abstinent because *their use has impaired a critical brain circuit that allows them to transfer the desire to change into action*. Overcoming addiction is no small feat. Still, there is no addiction too great to overcome.

There are millions of people in long term recovery that are *so anonymous …* many still don't believe, at the core of their being, that it is possible to actually stop this seemingly generational curse. Happily, major efforts are underway to change this with messages of real hope… people living vibrant meaningful lives. This country has a long way to go, with many of our current treatments of addiction almost setting people up for failure.

It does cross my mind that Joe saying out loud to me *that I love him unconditionally* has merit in its self…especially if the base of his intimacy issues has been an *inability* to feel unconditional love. *Joe has been trying to tell me from the very beginning that he wants and needs a friend!* He has a severe, complex, and prolonged history of addiction. No brief, low intensity treatments *initiating* recovery will probably lead right to the happy ever after for him. And I know…

"One must be careful when carrying light to the community to not leave one's own home in darkness" (-author unknown).

I get that… *I do.*

Yet…I sit here in this comfortable house *because a person suffering from chronic homelessness himself* went out of his way to see to it that *I* didn't end up that way. I've seen him give away his gloves to homeless people many times. I could go on and on. The man has a Heart of Gold that has been *demonized by addiction that is still just plain too poorly understood.*

I've noticed that *what should be suggested about addiction* has been under new lights lately. The movie "Nebraska" took home many Academy Awards this year. My take on that movie: the guy's dad was an alcoholic. Ok. But he was also a person, a person *first* who also just happens to have a disease. Simply by being a person, he is entitled to the respect and dignity that is the innate right of every human being. Yet, "Flight" is another great movie of recent times. The powerful message here was that *the guy finally ended the lying he'd done for a lifetime.*

Both ends of the spectrum have been exposed for us to ponder. There is truth to both points, and I find myself vacillating sometimes… in circles. And I imagine others do to. Askance and almost crazy as this may appear, I don't really care. My goal is to remain true to my voice as it unfolds. Letting reality be heard, at least, *makes for more informed thought processes.*

When my phone rings a few nights later, I am kind of surprised to see Joe's new number come up… I had started to think he was going to just hide out for years.

He thanks me for texting his daughter's phone number to him, but she hung-up when he tried to talk to her. He said he was *not going to let it get to him*, though I responded with an off-hand *you gotta take care of yourself* remark. He got defensive about it. I instinctively laid out enough of a deescalating tone that he started to settle back down …with a justifier statement that "I do really say some hurtful things sometimes."

He went on to example for me that the text I sent him about *being sorry I'd sent him money to come back…because now he may have missed his chance to bottom out…*hurt really bad .

"Anymore bottom for me at that point could only be death."

He tries again to *insist he was headed home, broke down, trying to get it fixed, and only headed in the other direction when I sent that text.*

"Well, I'm sorry. I was mad too. I found out your Dad had just talked to you on Bergen's phone, and you had went the opposite direction. *I believe* you were very sincere about coming back to go to treatment *until* you had to wait almost the whole day for me to get that money order figured out. I'm truly sorry. I don't know how to transmit things from Wal-Mart because I've never done it before. Plus, I'd went to a meeting that morning and I forgot to put my phone ringer back on…so I missed all your calls.. I'm sure that was so aggravating …*that's* when you probably decided …*fuck-it* …and headed in the opposite direction."

I hear him exhale with no further attempts to justify his position.

Then, I just talk to him about what's new in my life lately. I'm hoping to get an interview for a case management position at a faith-based center. I have spent time lately boning up on the more successful recovery programs. My job search is looking better now that I've completed my Master's degree. He is genuinely proud of me for this accomplishment.

I tell him I probably bombed my last interview because I was really late. I got lost trying to find a parking space in the thick of the downtown area…I have an impaired sense of direction as you know. Here, he gave a sympathetic response. Live and learn, they say.

He tells me *it just breaks his heart* about the dog. I tell him about *going to pick the dog up…* from the law enforcement's storage place on a Sunday. I made arrangements to meet the officer and follow him through a recycling complex… to a building with a big freezer in it. The officer was super nice. He went in and brought the dog out to me, and he looked pretty good all in all. I wrapped plastic over him and then a really nice blanket around him and put him in the trunk. I didn't want to even try to keep the emotion at bay.

So…*completely welled up and choking to breathe…* I got in the car and took off driving away. Tears are just streaming down when I realize I must have taken the wrong road back to the highway because all I can see is a great big compost dumping site. So, I turn around and come back to the freezer building. I discovered that the road I should have taken out of there… now has a big locked gate swung over it. I drive up and down a few more dead-end roads… in this recycling complex… feeling overwrought with our dead frozen dog in the trunk before I give up. *Finally, I have to call a dispatcher to send someone to come unlock the gate and get me out of there.*

Joe literally snorts out a convulsing laugh. "Only you," he says. "This could not happen to anyone but you."

"I know. I just can't figure out how I can do stuff like that either."

"It must be your ADHD or *something*."

"Well, he's home in the basement now anyway. Are… you planning to come back any time soon?" *I ask cautiously.* I go on to tell him about the early summer burial plans I'm making and that he's welcome to participate.

He tells me he's tentatively thinking of coming back at the end of April when his truck tabs are due…that he's thinking of *just giving me the truck in payment for all I've done for him.*

This takes me by surprise. I stammer around trying to suggest he just park it and go through a decent treatment program that helps him clean up his money issues. Then I hedge around about the latest recovery philosophies and managed to get it out how *we don't need to pray addicts will hit their bottom soon…what we need to do… is to offer hope!*

He heartily agreed with that statement.

I go on about food addiction being pretty tough too… how many times I'd joined programs to try to get them to teach me how to at just one cookie. This, of course, I cannot do… because it sets up a physical craving in me that I cannot stop. Typical weight loss programs could be aware of this phenomenon in addicts… *but since they make money on these programs…it's possible that they don't care.* Now …I *see* that certain trigger foods just have to be total abstinence, and still I screw up and have to start over time and time again.

On this note, Joe comes in with *that is right, that is what you have to do.* I know he is following what I'm talking about. He relays his elaborate knowledge and experiences with the health care system not finding better solutions to addictions. It has crossed my mind several times what a powerful advocate he would be for the New Recovery Movement's efforts to change the public's perception of what is actually needed for addiction recovery.

I managed to slip in the point that no one ever calls a diabetic *a low-life* … when they slip up, eat wrong, and go into insulin shock or something… and then wrapped the conversation up. It was getting late, and Joe had already had a long tiring day at work. He'd been sitting in his truck the whole time because the home he's staying at is pretty full of a lot of loud Mexicans talking to each other. He'd *call in a few days and he loves me.*

I am grateful to God to have Joe in my life. *He still opens my eyes.* Even though I do see addiction as a disease, I *had* fallen into shaming him with that text *about bottoming out.*

In my mind, a *good* treatment plan does seem like the best bet for him. But it is a decision he needs to come to by himself. He needs to live his own life.

Throughout this entire chronicling, I have tried diligently to show a 3D picture of addiction. There is a gal in my neighborhood, by the way, with fingernails over a foot long. I've heard this causes such interference in her life… some guy has to even wipe her butt for her. Yet…she semi- functions in her dysfunction. She has a job. She is friendly. Her grandkids sit on her lap and paint the fingernails for fun, etc. My first reaction was that by now… someone should have just wrestled her down and cut those claws off years ago. Why did they just stand by and let her ruin her life with such? Evidently, somehow, someway… it is providing some internal security or something.

So be it. I *do* believe that *effective* change has to come from the person *themselves* admitting that their life has become unmanageable and that they need a power greater than themselves to restore them to sanity.

Sadly, so much of the whole world is suffering with the pain of some sort of addiction because we've *been socialized to think that our minds will discipline us,* even though in reality… history is full of nations becoming indifferent to God and then… dying.

And… *here we are again* with any number of ways to try to use our minds to displace God as the creative intelligence that he is. But we don't really know how to live life on life's terms without some kind of painkiller. We can't see that *distress is woven in the fabric of this world,* and God is the way to lift above our circumstances.

I am thankful to be so far gone that I *have* to depend on God to survive. I am grateful for everything that has brought me to this point. Regardless of how many times I've fallen, I am always welcome to come back and try again. The only requirement for 12 step program is the *desire* to want to get better. Plus, we are never too far gone for *God's* mercy. Thank you, Jesus!

He called again last night…I had my phone within reach, too…right while I was taking a nice hot bath. The conversation started out with local news, but it got real pretty fast. He asked if his family was disgusted with him.

"I think everyone's frustrated with the disease itself and don't know what to do about it."

"Ya…*I can see that*…I feel the same way about it myself."

"I've been thinking about you and the whole *recovery* scene," I say in my upfront way.

"*Oh*…" was stated in such a way, I knew it was okay to continue on this thread.

I went on to share with him that *all the latest research predicts the way alcoholism is treated will make a dramatic shift in this next decade.*

He does then admit to me that he *is not at all happy and has even been wondering if he has another try at sobriety in him…he doesn't know what to do.* But he is willing to listen, and he lets me share whatever I can to try to offer hope.

"Ya… well… I'm older than you are, and I don't *want* to think that way at all. I want to believe that I can be a model of recovery for all those people that have suffered with addiction for a long, long time but then finally do find long term abstinence."

His "*Ok*…" makes me feel like he might be coming around a little more, so I go on.

I remind him that even *the way he tries to stay away, at least, from hard liquor, etc., indicates that he does not exactly have a death wish. Plus, I've always suspected that he short circuits his money supply sometimes just to save himself from the availably of too much using… that he is not looking to totally destroy himself… as much as he is self-medicating. But… he also needs to get in a good program that will help him heal the emotional hurts that he is so stuck on.*

He tolerated all of this, and then even *said maybe he'd try to save up enough money to come back in 2-3 weeks and consider a better treatment plan and that he'll try to call every night… and he loves me.*

"I love you too. I have struggled with my role with you… but know that I am your friend."

"I do know that."

I am content with the conversation. I have accepted the facts of this situation and then decided what I want to do about it. This is *not* the same as submitting to degrading. I have asked the hard questions here and received the gentle answers. Redemption, grace, and hope are just words… unless we make them *real*.

I have also again read through more of the new thinking about treatment programs. Success does look very promising "particularly for the alcoholic whose life hasn't completely deteriorated and who still has some intact social support."

So…yes…I can be his friend.

As I look back on this journal from only a few months ago, I discover that I prayed this: "*Dear God, fill me with your perspective until I joyfully lay down my will for yours.*" Somehow, I feel that it is being answered now with the direction I was looking for.

I pray to be used for the greater good, and I am thankful to have a heart for the hurting. I am so thankful now to have learned that waiting on God is the way we have been designed to live. Many blessings are promised to those that do wait on God: renewed strength, living above our circumstances, and… *the resurgence of hope.*

CHAPTER ELEVEN

On a Monday evening in mid-April, I received a call to contact Joe at a hospital in Nashville. The number they gave me didn't work, so I called his cell-phone. He answered. I learned that his drinking has again reached its *round-the-clock* level. He had blacked out in his truck. He went through a car-wash, down a ravine, and stopped in a play house. No one was hurt, but the officer brought him to the hospital to get checked out anyway... before taking him to the county jail. The truck is totaled.

I asked Joe to put me on the line with the officer. We had a long, polite, and serious conversation. I explained that Joe was a chronic alcoholic and *really* needed to be detoxed. The officer *assured* me that they had a wonderful pro-gram at their facility for this. Joe would be taken care of... the truck would go to an impound lot, and his court date would probably come up on Thursday.

Early the next morning, *they just let him out on the street.*

Joe called me from a phone he borrowed from a guy on the street. He was *ready to come back and go into treatment.* It would be at least a 14 hour drive, so he was contemplating hitchhiking back...or maybe I could meet him halfway. He'd figure it out and call me back as soon as he bought more minutes for his phone.

Then....no contact at until mid-morning Friday... when Joe left a message on my phone *that he definitely needed me to come get him... if I could.*

Joe had been released from the jail and then spent the last three days in an alarming stupor. One day, he had even gotten a hold of thirty Zantacs and had to be carried out of a bar. He spent his nights in the woods behind the bar, since he now had no vehicle to get out to the place he'd been staying. He'd drug a sleeping bag to a good spot… so drunk at times… he said he alternated lying down for a bit, then he would lean against a tree just to breathe.

I know how progressive this disease is, and that he is at point now where he is physically *unable* to go without alcohol. I am *horrified* that the officer promised to get him through a detox…but instead just let him go… *in a condition that really should be seen as a kind of Vulnerable Adult Violation.* I am sad there is such a long way to go still…to really get people the help they need. I amazed that he is even still alive.

I had already decided I would help him…so it was easy to try to do it with a good attitude. However, I decided not to get him *all* sobered up until I could get him in the safety of a detox center. If we'd see an emergency room before we got back… so be it. Thank God I had a great income tax return this year. I stopped for the night halfway and then pulled into Nashville around 3 pm on Saturday… just as planned. He called then from another borrowed phone to let me know where he was. It was just a short drive away.

I spotted Joe on the sidewalk bench… long before he saw me. He looked *so* distressed. His lovely posture now curled inward. He was not looking up. That reddened look of high blood pressure…with the coughing and shaking. I parked the car. I walked up to him and stood there until he did look up. Then I see all the pain and suffering in his face I ever want to see. It took him a moment to realize it was me, but I knew he would hug me *so good*… and he did.

I hear "I love you and you need to believe it… I am addicted to Bergen, and I'm working through it. But you do need *to know* that I *love* you. I know *now* that you were a*lways just trying to love me… and I just kept pushing you away.* I am ready to go get some help. I don't have any way to pay you either."

"Just get some real help this time…instead of those *spin-dry* places. That's all I want. It's payment enough." We are crying. I'm sure that I'm smearing snot around…but I don't care.

He had been staying with people that drank a lot… but they also cooked pretty decent Mexican food, so he wasn't skinny. The manual labor of painting was keeping him toned pretty well too. Plus, he'd had a buddy take him back to the place he'd been staying, so he could get cleaned up…before he walked down to this bench. It really was just so great to see him, no matter what.

As soon as we got in my car, I offered him bottled water. He hesitated for a moment, but then told me he really needed beer. I understood. The impound lot was closing soon so first we got the stuff from truck… clothes and a few tools. I met some of the Mexicans he'd been working with. I got to see some of the big projects he's been on *and* then we got him *lubricated up* again…a little bit.

He jokes with the guys, "Ain't she pretty?"

"Don't be trying to get on my good side, because I don't have one," I reply, and this brings the expected chuckles.

I let *that* ride. We decided to spend the night at a motel there in Nashville. He only wanted one bed. When we got in the room, he asked if I *wanted some of him…*

"No…nothing personal…but I want to be God's Will."

"I totally get it, and that's why I love you…I'm good with that." We cuddled on the bed and talked really honest while we waited for a cab to go out on the town.

I told him that the things we needed to work on… *that I was always secretly hoping we'd just get back to a Godly environment where Christian men came alongside him and mentored him through these issues… I didn't think it was my place to do it.* Then, we even touched on the issue of his attraction to petite women.

"I can remember way back when some scuzzy looking gal that worked at a junk store *oh what a big girl…* when you introduced me in a bar… and you couldn't handle it."

I saw that this was registering, so I went on. "It seems to be something you couldn't get past. I wasn't even 10 pounds overweight at that time. Prior to that comment…you thought I was pretty hot. So, I don't really believe my weight is the true issue here. It's like you are always running some kind of image control tape in your head…where any offhand comment…*from anyone really*…can dictate how you feel about something."

Incidentally, *that* bar scene happened over five and a half years ago. I'd *never* discussed it with him… yet, I was now very aware that he knew exactly what I was talking about. *And…* I can remember other times where this type of thing has occurred with us. Like once, he brought up some bone of contention over a biking accident we had, for the first time, many years afterwards… *and I knew exactly what he meant.* Another time when I lashed out, *long after the fact,* about his not letting me have *five minutes* to finish up a mowing project… I knew *he knew… exactly* what I was talking about.

*Sometimes, the connection between us is just off the charts…*then again, this might have something to do with how addicts know first-hand how long people can carry around even *minor* resentments.

His "I know it… I do have work to do… I couldn't even make it in a relationship for one month with a thin women…" came off pretty sincere.

Then, he went into how *nobody* else would have come to get him… that he *knows I love him unconditionally.* He *now* realizes that he loves me back unconditionally *just because of it.* I believe this is genuine…at least for his current mood. After all…isn't that why we love Jesus… because He *first* loved us?

Joe tell me that he wants nothing more than *to love and respect me… more than anyone.* I let him know that I did want to be cherished. I snuck in that *we have to really love God before all others* here too…to make sure I wasn't being put on a pedestal I couldn't live up to. I know I have a way to go, especially with the Bergen scene.

Several times now, he has shared that she was always jealous because he referred to me as his *best friend.* Yet, on the other hand, he believed they were akin to the *perfectly matched set.* I assume at least part of it was size-wise.

I contemplate informing him that *I* was attracted to a guy I worked with that I could easily project as the perfect body-style for me…*totally into me … and recovery…* and yet in the end… when he told me he *felt I still love Joe…*I let the whole thing go… *because he was right! I didn't tell* Joe things because it could factor out like intentionally causing jealousy… while we are in such a fragile state.

Anyway… the cab came. Out on the town, we went. It was grand to dance with him again. I felt myself grinning from ear to ear…with my eyes closed like some shyly happy little school girl…just to laugh and be with him again. We chatted with friendly people in the bars, and Joe was completely upfront about his situation.

I did feel kind of uncomfortable when he gushed too much about the *nobility* of my coming to get him. Because in reality… I know it is just a praise for God… doing His work *through* me.

I knew even to send bus money *at this point* would be too tempting for him to just get by with a few more highs. Plus, the system is still too ignorant to recognize how close to as seriously critical state he was in. Alas… they had just turned him out on the street without a care if he'd survive.

So, then Easter Sunday morning, we awake together and watch Joel Osteen in the motel room. My new Nashville guitar dress fits me fine. *Halleluiah…* Jesus is alive and well. After getting the rest of his things at the house where he'd been staying, we head back. We got lost often and just took our time. I was able to adjust and get comfortable with not being in such a hurry.

I am starting to realize that this is a big area in my life that God is working on with me. The *need to slow down and take is as it comes instead of the hell-bent to get through it and on to the next thing* type of *attitude* I seem to adhere to… I need to approach life by doing the right thing in the right way….not just the fastest way. And…I need to trust God that he will take care of me for operating this way.

We had in-depth conversations. Joe made a gallant effort to work through some things verbally. "Boy, those Mexicans taught me so much about searching for the women with the *heart*…go for the *heart* they said. Did you notice how big Miguel's wife is? *They* know better than to go for the arm candy."

When we decide to stop for the night, the motel gal recommended a nice supper club. We struggled to find it but *finally* did. I am ready for a nice steak dinner… for sure. Joe decide margarita and a shot… over and above his beers. I don't want to argue at this point…so whatever.

When we got back to the room, he was just crying out in pain… saying his lower kidney area was so inflamed and swollen that it was almost unbearable. I consider finding a hospital right then and there. But then he drops off to sleep with the loudest rattling snore I have ever heard come out of him. I managed to drift off... but *I wake to a start* when I realize that it is *deathly quiet* in the room. *Joe is not making any sound at all.*

I am in a trance, wondering if he's *dead*. I don't want to touch him... *in case he's not and I wake him up.* I am laying there trying to decide what to do when... *thank-you, Jesus*... he does wake up. I tell him how hard he was snoring *and then* when he got completely quiet... I was scared.

"That's what Bergen used to say... that I'd *start off* snoring but I'd quiet down after a while. But she snored too. It was so cute. I used to love just laying there and listening to it."

I know that he is drunk and trying to be in some happy place in his head. He was so infatuated with her that I can see these thoughts are going to take some time to go away. But... I am now seemingly propelled by pure instinct. Okay...yes...I came unglued.

"I do not want to hear the name again. I am not willing to tolerate it. I can't even tell you the levels of stupid you are...but you are STUPID! I don't think you say things like that to hurt me on purpose... I believe that you are just that stupid." I find myself clapping my hands together in a very loud staccato rhythm... accenting my words.

I take a breath, and the second verse rise up. "My God... you borrow my grill to do your big impress scene so you can fuck that piece of shit! Then... I drive by to try to get it, and I see a brand new grill in your yard that I'm pretty sure ended up at her place... and I never did even get mine back..." And on and on.

He may have tried to utter some kind of defense here, but I hit the clap on my hands again so hard, he stopped cold. I go on. "You're so far into your addiction that you can't even see that you don't have the right to buy shit for other people when you still owe other people money. And then you don't have the brains not to rub my nose in your lovesickness besides. You are SOOOO... STUPID!!!" And then I add, "Plus... one of the biggest reasons you got into this mess in the first place... and you don't even realize... is because YOU AND I have such a fucked-up relationship. God, you need so much help!"

"Okay," he half whispers. "calm down."

I find comfort in the fact that it is dark enough that we can't see each other. Even though I am certainly wound up and threw a curveball from hell square at him… I am… surprisingly calm.

I do worry that he may think I really care about the money he owes me… when in fact I really want him to stop throwing his money around when he has bills to pay. I am able to get back to sleep…thankfully. Probably because I am more than aware that this is going to be a long process and never perfect… so just accept it. He apologized the next morning with, "You are right …I am stupid… really, really stupid."

"Well, you're actually not…but you really do some stupid stuff" comes softly out of my mouth.

"So, are we going to have a good day?"

"I feel pretty good… so if you can get a little smarter…we should be okay." Joe scoffs a little, and I can change the subject.

"When deep injury is done to us, we never recover until we forgive. Forgiveness does not change the past…it enlarges the future." -Mary Karen Reed

From there, we detour over to visit his oldest sister, who he hasn't seen for many years. Even though it's a good half day away…it is the right thing to do. Joe may never get a chance to see her again. I am glad we visited because I learn a lot from this impromptu family gathering. Regardless of some very severe wrong doings…some very real recovery has also been taking place in their immediate family… even a few generations forward now. Praise God, and good to know.

Actually, it reminds me of the biggest lesson I ever learned in my life. I had been so beaten down with my drug addiction 15 years ago…that I had to discover a new way to live and think. And you can believe that I was hanging on to my right to have big resentments. I am an incest survivor for Christ sake. Surely that is so heinous… it is not to be forgiven.

Yet, there I was wallowing around in an affair with a married man, who had been supplying my drugs for 10 years. My reasons were justifiable, of course… life was hard and unfair, and I had to cope somehow to survive.

The thing is, it wasn't until I could come to terms with the level of sin that had been forgiven of me…that I could forgive the level of sin that had be done onto me. Once I could see how much alike we all really are, I made some progress in my ability to forgive things.

We can all get to the point where we are in such a sick place that nothing is sacred anymore… our only concern is getting those sick needs met…regardless of how sick they are. It just manifests out differently per situation.

Even when Joe talks about things like paddle boating with Bergen… which we used to do . . . or when I realize that he didn't manage to save the painting I made of his dad and him…let alone subjecting me to their intimate details… my heart just slices open.

It's like nothing is sacred to him. I am tempted to deem these things at a level of disrespect… that should not be forgiven, but I've decided to work through it. Maybe someday, if he realizes how others can manage to forgive him, he can start to forgive himself. Then … maybe he can start to really forgive the people that have deeply hurt him, and a new level of wellness will descend.

The question for me really becomes how do I learn to forgive wholly and completely?

So far, I know that the true feeling of forgiveness is a gift from above that I have had to learn, over and over again, how to receive.

In order for healing to really work, I need to flip the switch and release the power that governs it. I need to draw close to God so I can truly learn to do the right things in love, and I can only do that if my heart is right. Some days, I do really have to fight to keep my faith. Yet I know that faith is the only thing that conquers my fears. I pray to be informed about what God wants my part to be and to NOT be afraid of the future.

Part of being saved is to gain a better understanding of ourselves and others. How I go about this is a form of my creativity. It is my individual expression… individual just like how we are all created individually.

One way for me to release the power I need to make this happen is to say it out loud in this work right here: "I do choose to dwell in the shelter of God, the Most High." God is with me here; I feel it.

So, we went on driving back. We took a few more wrong turns and some neat back roads. Yes, we stopped at some quaint taverns, too… a rather relaxing trip all in all. We got home on Tuesday. Joe needed a day to adjust. I'd saved the mail that continued to come here for him, so he was resolute to dig into the pile and assess the damages.

Lo and behold… and miracle upon miracle…the child support bill has been dropped! Back in the late seventies, when this first came about, Joe was to pay the original hospital bill only. The women's new husband adopted the baby, and Joe didn't even get visitation. At one point, he had it paid down to less than $200's. Then when this bill re-appeared to raise its ugly head, it was over $14,000's… with all the accrued interest tacked on. He had gotten an attorney last summer finally to look into it but lost track of it when he left.

The attorney had discovered that all old cases under $500's were to be deemed closed. WOW! WOW! WOW! This had been the major stumbling block for him even getting a driver's license back! Unbelievable as it seemed… we went down to the license bureau to have his record checked, and sure enough…it is marked as satisfied. God loves Joe so much, and we both know it.

He did a detox program and was out and feeling so much better in a few days. They used valium to bring him down, and it worked well. He says it just feels so wonderful to be out from under the constant burden to have to find a way… to get his next buzz.

Things ticked off like clock-work. He was accepted for the 90-day Life Renewal Program and will get in soon. I offered to give him bus money to go to an AA meeting during the day . . . he declined. "I don't want to get in a situation out there in public and be tempted to use." I know he wants to stop forever, and I believe that with the right programming, he will be able to.

Saturday, I scored a very nice French Lilac Bush for free from craigslist. Joe persisted with the extremely tough job of digging it up until he did get it to come up nicely, and we have it in the yard now. We also dug the grave for the dog and buried him in the back yard. The spot is perfect with a little of the lilac bush in front and a small dog statue I painted to look like our baby… as Joe calls him.

"I loved that dog," he said in a breaking up voice. I was so glad he was here to help me do it. It just couldn't be any other way.

I worked my temp jobs during the day, and Joe hugged and kissed me off to work with words of "Oh, you look so pretty." He worked though his credit report and everything he could gather up to take into treatment to start straightening things out. We thoroughly enjoyed watching several great movies together and even cuddled on the couch. It was sweet and beautiful.

He happened to throw out the word exploit for no reason I could see. So, I said, "Really…that was the thing that used to burn me the most… when you would accuse me of exploiting you."

He answered back, "Well, that's the alcoholic in me. I'm so used to being exploited that I can't believe there's anyone that not doing it to me."

I was pretty impressed with the insight and honesty in that statement. He also even owned up to his crack using which I'd asked him about last summer. He had denied it at the time. Now, just out of the blue, he acknowledged that too.

So, I felt the need to be honest myself. "Well…I do have something I need to tell you about that book I was writing. Actually, I got enough of an income tax return to just go ahead and self-publish. In fact, the proofs are already here. But they have also conceded to let me add another chapter."

Joe is nodding approval along with this, so I decide to go for broke here. "Anyway, before …you were mad about it, I know. Please understand that I have gone way out of my way to not disclose identities. I don't ever want you to feel like I am exploiting you."

I hand him the cover to look at as I say all of this to him. Surprisingly, he responds with, "It's alright… I admit, at first, I was really mad…but then I thought it through, and now I feel rather honored. I really like the cover too."

I went on talking about ways to market it anonymously. Now he doesn't really seem to care about that too much, but I do. I believe that anonymity is a very good tool here, and God will provide the right market for it. Meanwhile, I am happy to at least finally have Joe's blessing on this undertaking.

One night, we went to a great AA meeting. Joe really got into his story. It was powerful. I know the newcomer there heard exactly what he needed to hear. I am so proud of him. I felt like the Joe I hadn't seen in a long time was really back. "The best rescuers are those that have been rescued."

I know there will always be problems… but God will equip me to handle them as I go. Really…I did land a decent case management job now, and that is the field I want to get into. I am closer and closer to my goal weight. I love working with my new sponsor on my 12- step program.

Joe is now in a treatment program that has a very impressive success rate for individuals that have failed at other programs. Almost all of them credit this to the faith-based piece of the programming. It's a nice facility, and they treat people respectfully.

Somehow, it has to be different for him this time. My heart just breaks when I look at photos his boss in Nashville texted to me. One is when they were working on him to bring him back from overdosing and another one where they had found him passed out …laying on a sidewalk…with leaves blowing around him. I cannot describe how disturbing those pictures are.

Joe did now get on medication to relieve his depression and got some nicotine patches. He is in a safe place. God will work on him. I take comfort in hearing him say things now like, "whether or not the steps work perfectly for me…I know they are based on Biblical truths…so that's what I'm mining now."

I pray to just take it one day at a time and diligently continue to work my own program. Al-anon has taught me to sort out my good qualities and build a strong foundation on them. For starters, I realize that I am, at least, tenacious.

Joe has said we will follow whatever God's Plan for our lives…becomes laid out to us. So, for starters, I'm going to share this story. I hope I can show enough about humility, honesty, and fearlessness to help others discover another level of real recovery, too.

Alas, it is a way for me to be an open vessel for change. I see this format as a valuable expression where people can gain knowledge and understanding of others. It's an avenue where specific populations can be reached… in a manner they can relate to. Literary non-fiction is a very effective way to explore and capture the atmosphere and experiences of real people, and thus, a very important area to continue to research. Exposure to people in recovery… shows us how many addicts… actually can go on to live wonderful meaningful lives.

I am respecting both of our rights to privacy, while, at the same time, presenting very useful literature. It is a tool for viewing addiction and recovery in many lights. We are also in an era where it much easier for individuals to share personal stories to broad audiences. And, it can be emulated as a therapeutic approach for others… to journal through their trials.

I've heard it said that the shortest distance between human beings…to the truth… is a true story. Everyone's personal story has value and certainly adds to the pool of wisdom … gained from life experiences.

Stories show us what happens between our intentions and then the end results. Current therapy teaches that sharing and reflecting on life events offers great personal benefits …even if it's only just to really take a good look at something and then move on.

And finally, we are creating a culture that is calling for transparency as an important functioning level in the treatment of addiction. In the recovery rooms, there's no shame in sharing…only healing. I'm hoping to take it a little farther out.

God Bless you all… each and every one. He does you know.

ABOUT THE AUTHOR

Jolene Jones holds a Master's Degree in Human Services and a Certificate in Addiction Counseling. She has spent more than 30 years in the Human Service Field. This work is her writing debut as an artist exploring the private spaces of the mind and heart. Jolene lives in the United States of America and is using this as her pen-name to respect the nature of the subject material.